COBRA FILES

Case no. 20-8-5/13-15-12-5-19/

23-8-15/3-1-13-5/9-14/6-18-15-13/

20-8-5/3-15-12-4

Operation: Misbehaving Moles

Status: **TOP SECRET**

For Sam xx

OXFORD
UNIVERSITY PRESS

Great Clarendon Street, Oxford OX2 6DP

Oxford University Press is a department of the University of
Oxford. It furthers the University's objective of excellence in
research, scholarship, and education by publishing worldwide.

Oxford is a registered trade mark of Oxford University Press
in the UK and in certain other countries

British Library Cataloguing in Publication Data

Data available

ISBN: 978-0-19-277364-7

1 3 5 7 9 10 8 6 4 2

Printed in India

Paper used in the production of this book is a natural, recyclable
product made from wood grown in sustainable forests. The
manufacturing process conforms to the environmental
regulations of the country of origin.

MICKEY

·:· AND THE ·:·

TROUBLE

WITH MOLES

ANNE MILLER

Illustrated by
BECKA MOOR

OXFORD
UNIVERSITY PRESS

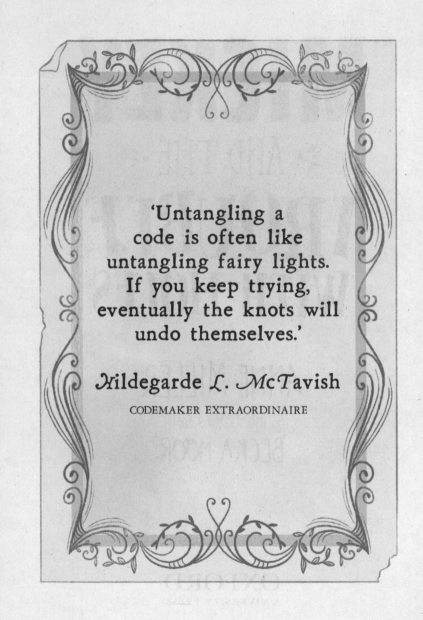

'Untangling a
code is often like
untangling fairy lights.
If you keep trying,
eventually the knots will
undo themselves.'

Hildegarde L. McTavish

CODEMAKER EXTRAORDINAIRE

Chapter

1

RAT-A-TAT-TAT.

Mickey sat bolt upright in her bed. **RAT-A-TAT-TAT** came the noise again. The strange sound seemed to be coming from her window.

She sprang out of bed and drew back the curtain to reveal a slightly soggy **rat** perched on the windowsill, paw raised to knock again. She looked down into the back garden of her block of flats, and by a mix of the dazzling moonlight and the soft lights of the city she could just make out the distinctive silhouette of a giraffe standing very still against the fence.

Some people might respond to being woken up in the middle of the night by a rat and a giraffe by quickly closing the curtains, pulling the duvet over their head and going straight back to sleep until morning. But Michaela Rose Thompson was not 'some people'. In some ways she was quite normal—she lived in a flat with her parents, she enjoyed school, and did gymnastics on Fridays. But in one very important way Mickey was actually quite extraordinary.

Mickey's favourite thing was cracking codes. During the summer she had spotted a hidden message on the bus and solving it had led to her being recruited by a top secret organisation of animal spies called **COBRA**. It was run by a cobra named Coby (who Mickey had just about managed to stop feeling frightened of). Aided by her trusty High Committee, Coby and her team were in charge of protecting the country's animals from dangers that humans couldn't even imagine. Over the summer Mickey had helped them solve a case involving a dognapper and a diamond thief and was now an important member of their group.

Agent profiles:

Mickey, Human:
Human Liaison Officer

Coby, Snake: Head of COBRA

Clarke, Cat:
Head of Domestic Affairs
(Head of Pets)

Rupert, Rat: Head of Wild Affairs
(Head of Wild Animals)

Astrid, Spider Monkey:
Head of International Affairs
(Head of International Animals)

Tilda, Sloth:
Temporary Member
(a post which rotates
between different animals)

Bertie, Giraffe: Security Guard

7

The rat sitting on her windowsill was Rupert, the Head of Wild Animals and one of Mickey's most trusted allies. The giraffe trying to hide his considerable height behind a tree was Bertie, the **COBRA** security guard who occasionally doubled up as their mode of transport as he had the longest legs and could get to places much faster than Tilda the sloth could on her own.

'Rupert!' Mickey called softly, fumbling with the catch on her window and pulling it up so he could crawl inside. 'Are you okay?'

'Terribly sorry to disturb you at this hour my dear,' replied the rat. 'We have a bit of a . . . situation and Coby asked me to collect you.'

Mickey was already zipping up a jacket over her pyjamas and reaching for her boots. 'I'm ready!' she said. 'What's happened?'

'It's the moles,' said Rupert. 'They've broken into a bank!'

Chapter 2

Mickey soon found herself on Bertie's back with Rupert perched in front of her as they zoomed through the dark streets towards their destination.

'The others are already on their way,'
Rupert explained. 'There wasn't much time
to warn you—I hope I didn't wake you too
abruptly, my dear.'

'Not at all!' said Mickey, clinging on tightly
to Bertie's neck as he ran. 'How serious is it?'

'Very,' replied the rat, his legs flying out
behind him as Bertie picked up speed. 'Coby
is furious. She's hoping it's just one mole who
has tunnelled in by mistake . . .'

'It *is* hard to tell when you're
underground,' added Bertie. 'I imagine,
anyway. Everywhere must look the same.'

'Very true, very true,' mused Rupert.

The bright lights of the city sped past in a
blur as Bertie galloped along but he stuck
to the shadows and quiet lanes, avoiding the
main roads which were full of cars even at
this late hour. It was almost hypnotic and
coupled with the rhythmic movement of
the running giraffe Mickey worked to keep
her eyes open and was relieved when Bertie

finally called 'We're here!' and pulled to a
stop inside a narrow lane with a cobbled
pavement.

Mickey felt herself jolt forward and quickly
grabbed hold of Rupert so he didn't fall off. It
would feel much more of a drop to the ground
if you were a rat. One side of the lane was
edged with rough grassland and opened onto
the common which Mickey liked to walk on
with her parents. The other side was lined
with a neat brick wall, and a heavily secured
gate led into the service yard for the biggest
bank in the city—The United Bank. The grey
stone building stretched up over three floors
and had four gleaming chimneys erupting
from the roof.

Ready to explore, Mickey was just about
to jump down when a flash of white paws
appeared at the top of the wall surrounding
the bank and she spotted Clarke, the feline
Head of Domestic Affairs (pets).

'There you are, come on!' he called by way
of greeting.

Bertie shuffled closer to the wall so Mickey

and Rupert could clamber across to join Clarke on the wall, before shrinking back towards the opposite side of the lane where he disguised himself as a slightly oddly-shaped street light.

'Where are we going?' Mickey whispered.

'This way!' said Clarke, nodding his head towards the bank's main building. 'And watch your balance!'

Mickey, who was not a natural athlete, thanked her lucky stars for her gymnastics lessons after school. Following Clarke, she tucked Rupert inside her jacket pocket and felt him snuffle around as he checked for forgotten biscuit crumbs, while she concentrated on keeping her balance as the team moved along the wall.

'The others are already up there,' Clarke whispered over his shoulder.

'Up where?' asked Rupert from inside Mickey's pocket.

'The roof,' said Clarke. 'You need to jump for this bit.'

Mickey watched nervously, as Clarke sprang from the wall to a metal fire escape which zigzagged its way up the outside of the building. 'We're not supposed to be up here!' she whispered, fearful for what would happen if they got caught. 'It's the middle of the night and this is trespassing.'

Mickey couldn't see his features in the dark but knew Clarke was rolling his eyes.

'It would be much worse if we didn't do

anything. The moles are running amok inside and it's only a matter of time before they set off an alarm. If we meet on the ground we might be seen or overheard but on the roof we can speak freely.'

Operating in secret was one of **COBRA**'s most important rules. Coby said that if people knew what animals were capable of it would make it much harder for them to get on with their missions. The only people who knew about **COBRA** were Mickey and their previous Human Liaison Officer Harry. He nearly destroyed all faith **COBRA** had left in humans when he had switched sides and started working against **COBRA**, and as a result Mickey had had to work extra hard to persuade the High Committee that not all humans were untrustworthy.

'How do we get up there without being seen?' asked Rupert, who was looking around to scan the area for security cameras.

'Coby had some of the seagulls fly by and take some well-aimed toilet breaks. The cameras on this side won't be capturing anything new until they've been cleaned. The others are already up there—hurry up!' hissed Clarke.

Satisfied that she wouldn't have to explain to the police, or worse her parents, why she'd been found lurking around a bank with a rat, a cat, and a giraffe, Mickey took a deep breath and decided to follow Clarke. She jumped across to the metal stairs on the fire escape, landing as quietly as she could. Clarke was already starting to disappear again so she picked up her pace and flew up the stairs after him, keeping her tread as soft as possible, just in case someone was listening. As she came to the top she saw the white of Clarke's paws disappear as he sprang up onto the roof.

Mickey knew she couldn't spring like a cat no matter how many hours she poured into gymnastics, so she stretched out her hands and ran them over the wall looking for footholds before realizing that even better, there was an old drainpipe. Carefully, she reached out to give it a shake to test it and thankfully it seemed still and sturdy. Looking up, she calculated the roof wasn't more than a few metres away and decided she could make it. Methodically, she moved hand over hand, pulling herself up until finally she was up on the roof.

'Phew!' said Rupert, as he leapt out of her pocket, and looked around at the view while fanning himself with his front paw. 'That was quite the climb.'

Mickey was fond of Rupert so decided against pointing out that she had done all the hard work. In fact, she was trying quite hard not to think too much about how high up they were. She'd found herself in various scrapes since joining **COBRA** but never before had she found herself on the roof of a bank in the middle of the night. The wind whipped around and blew her hair into her face as she leaned against a nearby chimney to steady herself.

Suddenly the silhouettes of the rest of the **COBRA** High Committee came into focus on the rooftop in front of her—contrasting neatly

against the shining moonlight.
She could see the long-limbed
shape that was Astrid's shadow,
and the rounder shadow which
belonged to Tilda the sloth.
Also coming towards them,
head raised, was Coby, the
cobra in charge of **COBRA**.

'Ssssssso, you made it,' she
hissed in greeting.

Chapter

3

'Greetings, Mickey,' Coby continued. 'Thank you for joining us so late at night.'

'Are the moles still in there?' Mickey asked, gesturing downwards.

'They are,' said Astrid the spider monkey, 'though they've managed not to set the human alarms off so that's something.'

'Indeed,' said Clarke, 'although what they think they're doing breaking into a bank I have no idea. I have numerous matters to take care of at night and this is taking me away from my important cat business.'

'Just a reminder,' puffed Tilda who was usually slightly behind the rest of the group, even over short distances, 'the moles haven't set any alarms off *yet* but we need to remove them from the bank and find out what they're up to fast. Every minute that passes increases the risk of humans discovering both them and then us.'

'And that's going to be hard to explain,' Mickey mused. 'How do you know they're definitely inside the bank?'

'They made some noise when they tunnelled up through the floor which alerted the attention of another animal nearby who gave us a tip-off,' said Clarke with a swish of his tail. 'Oh, here he comes now.'

'Duck!' called Astrid.

As Mickey scanned the roof for the approaching duck all the others dropped to the ground. A fresh breeze suddenly tickled Mickey's face as a dark shadow came swooping silently towards her. But this was no duck, Mickey thought, as an almighty

'SCREEEEEEEEEECH'

filled the air. It was a beautiful barn owl, with bright eyes, a snowy white heart-shaped face and two graceful long round wings who came in to land on the top of the chimney pot before staring intensely at each member of **COBRA** in turn to see who was there. He tipped his head to one side when his eyes landed on Mickey, as if weighing up her presence.

'And who—ooh is this?' he asked.

'Screech,' said Coby, cutting in neatly. 'Let me introduce you to our Human Liaison Officer. This is Mickey.' She pointed neatly with her tail—rather unnecessarily, thought Mickey, as none of the others looked particularly human.

'Hello,' she said. Screech flapped his wings and politely held one foot out and Mickey shook it. 'What a funny name! Why do they call you "Mickey"?' he asked.

'Um, it's my name,' said Mickey. 'It's short for Michaela. And you must be called Screech because that's the call of a barn owl?'

'SCREEEEEEEEECH'

replied the barn owl, stretching his wings out to show off his impressive wingspan. The noise was so loud that Mickey's ears suddenly felt very hot and she noticed the other animals covering theirs up with their paws. She felt Rupert taking shelter behind her right boot.

'Screech, I have told you not to do that,' said Clarke crossly.

'You said that about *inside*, but we're outside now!' said the owl triumphantly, flapping his wings.

'Mickey replaced Harry after all that . . . unfortunate *business* this summer,' said Coby smoothly.

'It's unusual given she's not grown up yet but you'll find she is quite competent once you get to know her,' added Clarke.

Mickey tried not to grin as she knew that 'quite competent' was actually very high praise from the cat.

'I just flew by the window at the front of the building and the moles are still in there,' reported Screech. 'The other roof birds and

I would like them gone please. I have very sensitive hearing and they are causing a nuisance. Also, we owls quite literally like to fly under the radar and don't want the bank humans to start sniffing around and finding our homes. Not everyone likes to have birds on their roof.'

'I would!' said Mickey quickly. 'Do you know what the moles are doing?'

'I suppose you'd have to ask them,' Screech continued. 'But it appears they are searching for something. They're making quite a mess of the banking hall. But all is not lost—some of the birds may be able to recycle some of the papers they're destroying as nesting material.'

Mickey hoped it was just paper the moles were destroying and not money. She wondered briefly what the bank's security might do if they found out the nests of the city's bird population were being lined with £50 notes.

'How do we get inside to stop them?' Mickey asked.

Screech ruffled his beautiful feathers.

'Well,' he said, '*sometimes* a curious bird
might find a window slightly open and
just happen to fly in to have a look round.
However, we've checked and tonight they're
all locked and if you tamper with the door
an alarm goes off. However, there is another
option.' He paused dramatically for effect
like somebody announcing the winner on a
TV talent competition. 'The moles must have
tunnelled up through the floor but if you
wanted to take them by surprise you could
always go down a chimney. Not this one,'
he paused to tap the nearest chimney with
a talon, 'because it's boarded up, but *that*
one'—he pointed to the next chimney with his
wing—'leads down to the ground floor.'

Mickey walked over to the chimney and
looked down. All she could see was darkness.

'I think you'll fit,' said the owl, 'but it
might be a bit of a squeeze.'

Chapter

'Well, don't think I'll be going down there,' said Clarke. 'It looks filthy.'

'At least you always land on your feet,' said Tilda, looking worried.

'I should probably go as the moles are part of my remit—as Head of Wild Animals,' said Rupert as he looked anxiously down the chimney. 'The moles are my responsibility.'

Mickey looked at her animal spy colleagues, all of whom were suddenly very busy looking at the view from the rooftop and not at the long way down into the chimney. Mickey could see they didn't want to be the ones to climb and given her gymnastics training she knew what she could do.

'I'll do it!' she said.

'Thank you, Mickey,' said Coby smoothly. 'May I remind everyone that time is very much of the essence.' The snake paused to draw herself up to her full height. Coby was a large snake and knew that this move usually ensured her orders were followed *immediately*. 'Mickey, you have the longest arms and legs so are the best candidate to go down. Rupert, you can travel in Mickey's pocket and . . . well . . .'

Mickey's quick brain realized the snake wanted to see inside the hall too but wouldn't ask for help for fear of undermining her authority. So, Mickey decided to be kind.

'Of course,' she said, 'but Rupert's quite light so I could probably take someone else too, perhaps you or Astrid . . .'

'An excellent idea,' cut in Coby. 'I shall travel with you. Astrid, Tilda, and Clarke, please run surveillance on the grounds, entrances and exits—watch to see if any humans start arriving or moles start escaping. Screech, how do we enter via this chimney?'

'I'll show you,' said Screech. He soared up into the air then turned and dived down the chimney.

The animals turned and looked at Mickey expectantly.

'I can't do it like that,' she said quickly. 'But we can climb down.'

Carefully she secured Rupert into her pocket. Then Coby wound herself around Mickey's neck like a scarf as Mickey reached for the top of the chimney and slowly swung her legs over the top.

Even though it was the middle of the night Mickey couldn't help worrying that someone would light a fire underneath, but was reassured by the fact she could hear Screech hooting softly from below. She tried to distract her brain from thinking about how high up she was and the fact that if she fell she was risking not one, not two, but three lives from the **COBRA** High Committee—plus potentially Screech as well depending on how they landed. But then she remembered being taught at school that children really did used to be sent into chimneys to sweep them and she realized there must be a trick to it. She reached around with her legs and

suddenly the
left one found
a foothold. She
lowered her
right foot until
she found
another, then
lowered her
hands

down

the

chimney.

There were enough ridges that she could almost pretend she was climbing down a very uncomfortable ladder. However, the smell as she climbed down was quite overpowering. The chimney smelled like a bonfire that had burned for hundreds of years and then been left to smoke.

She wished she had a hand free to cover her mouth and nose but, as if reading her mind, Coby flicked her tail to pull Mickey's jacket up over her nose.

'Breathe through your mouth,' she hissed gently, 'it helps.'

'This way,' called Screech, as they finally reached the bottom and tiptoed into what looked like an abandoned office room. There was a large ornamental fan sitting in the fireplace which Mickey dodged around before hurriedly dragging it back into position, covering their tracks in case someone looked in.

'Remember to be-ee qui-eet,' Screech hooted gently as he gestured to the door of the room.

Mickey gently pushed the door open a crack

so they could peer into the main hall and assess the situation, and heard Rupert gasp from his place in her pocket.

The hall of the bank was full of moles running all over the place. Some were scuttling around the floor, others were attempting to climb the walls, one pair were rifling through a pile of papers which had been left on a desk and there was a hole in the floor just next to the front door there was a fire extinguisher lying on its side.

'This is outrageous!' said Coby. 'They must have made their tunnel just behind the fire extinguisher so no one would see the hole until after they'd made their attack!' That is quite clever, thought Mickey.

'I don't know what's got into them,' mused Rupert. 'It's far too risky for a prank, and they have no need to break into a bank— moles don't use money!'

'We must stop them!' said Coby.

'However you do it I'd move fast,' said Screech. 'It's only a matter of time until they trip the alarm. Look at those ones over there.'

He pointed to the
far corner of the room
where several moles were
arranging themselves
into a pyramid—like
human acrobats—with
another preparing to
climb on top of them
to reach the padlock
on a door marked
'PRIVATE'.

'This endsssss now,'
hissed Coby as she pushed
the door fully open with
her tail and slithered into the banking hall.

Mickey and Rupert were close behind, but
Screech hung back in the shadows.

'Stop this at ONCE!' cried the snake.

The room fell silent. All the moles froze
and it was so quiet you could have heard a
pen drop. Which Mickey did, as one of the
moles knocked one off a table.

Rupert stepped forward and scanned the
room.

'I don't believe it!' he said as he watched a mole scurry over to pick up the pen. 'Phyllis? Is that you?'

'Er . . . good evening Rupert?' the mole called Phyllis said sheepishly. She was small enough to fit into Mickey's palm, covered in dark velvety fur with a bright pink nose and front paws, one of which she waved casually to Rupert as if they'd met on the common to catch up rather than one finding the other mid break-in.

'What on earth are you doing?' he asked.

But Phyllis didn't have time to reply because suddenly there was a thud, then an 'oops' as the mole on top of the pyramid toppled over, right into a sensor on the door marked 'PRIVATE'. Suddenly, the room was filled with an ear-splitting noise as the bank's security alarm went off and smoke began to fill the banking hall.

'Everybody out—NOW!' said Coby. 'Moles, rat, human—GO!'

Mickey had read about smoke being used to stop thieves. It works by cloaking everything

in a thick
smoky fog—
the idea being that
anyone who had broken
in wouldn't be able to see
anything to steal it. But it
would also soon block the sight of the
exits. The moles, realising the alarms had
been activated and humans would be on
their way soon, began to scurry across the
room, making their way to the hole by the
front door which they poured through like
a stream. The smoke grew thicker. Mickey
started to struggle to see as the moles and the
room began to vanish from sight.

'They're getting away!' she cried.

'I'll follow them,' said Rupert quickly.

Mickey did not like the sound of Rupert
going after the moles alone, but she knew
there was no way she'd fit down the moles'
tunnel. 'Be careful,' she called.

'I will.' Mickey felt Rupert press his paw onto her left foot. 'I'll report back to HQ tomorrow.'

'Okay,' she reluctantly agreed. 'Take care!'

'I always do,' he replied, then Mickey heard his paws scampering and he was gone.

'We need to leave NOW,' Coby suddenly hissed into Mickey's ear. 'I'll lead.'

The smoke was getting thicker and Mickey

knew that smoke rises so having Coby low to the ground was a big advantage. Mickey crawled on her hands and knees after Coby until they reached the chimney, looped the snake around her shoulders then reached up again, climbing as though their lives depended on it. Hoping that Screech had flown up before them she climbed desperately, reaching for the ridges above her and pulling herself up with all her might until she could see the star-filled sky at the top of the chimney which meant safety.

Chapter 5

When she finally emerged with Coby safely tucked around her neck, she breathed deeply and took in great gulps of the delicious, fresh, smoke-free air. The other members of **COBRA** would be taking cover on the ground. They were all safe and so was Screech who came soaring overhead. 'Well done,' he called. 'Just lie flat. Security never think to search up on the roof for some reason—some humans just don't think outside the box!'

Mickey got the feeling Screech might have set off the bank's alarm before.

'Do you think all the moles got out?' she whispered as she lay down next to Coby. She suddenly felt the night-time chill now the warmth she'd generated by moving so quickly was starting to fade.

'Sssshould have,' hissed Coby, wriggling in next to her for warmth. Coby wasn't a cuddly creature but the cold made her slow down and Mickey had learned she liked to do things as quickly as possible. The sound of sirens whirred in the distance, growing closer by the second.

'Do you think Rupert made it to the tunnel in time?' she asked.

'He's very quick on his feet,' said Coby. 'He is probably questioning the moles and gathering intelligence as we speak.'

Mickey gazed out at the view over the city and watched the lights of the world below her until the piercing alarm stopped and Screech came to peck gently at her foot.

'Bank security are scratching their heads,' said Screech gleefully. 'They can't figure out why the place is in such a mess. The moles pulled the fire extinguisher back over the hole they made which is really quite clever, and it looks as though they managed to disable the

CCTV inside the bank too. Rather impressive! Anyway, they've given up for now and called it a false alarm, so you are free to go.'

Mickey gave herself a shake then began the climb back down to the alleyway where she was grateful to see Bertie waiting patiently, still disguised as a street lamp.

'Let's reconvene at HQ tomorrow at 11 a.m. to hear Rupert's report,' said Coby. 'Bertie, please will you take Mickey home?'

Now the excitement was over Mickey suddenly found herself feeling very sleepy (and rather grubby from her time in the chimney) so she was grateful for the ride back.

'Please don't fall off,' the giraffe said nervously as they prepared to leave. Mickey wrapped her arms around his neck and thanked her lucky stars it was still dark, so she was able to get home quickly on her unusual form of transport without being seen.

'Thanks, Bertie,' she whispered as he drew to a halt outside Mickey's building. As she crept up the stairwell and into her flat she could tell from the shoes in the hallway that her dad was home, but her mum was still at work. Her parents were scientists and were often working on experiments and projects at odd hours. Sometimes Mickey thought this made her unlucky as they weren't always around to eat dinners with or to come on school trips but sometimes it made her feel very lucky as she had lots of opportunities for her top-secret **COBRA** work. Tonight, it worked in her favour because her dad was by far the heavier sleeper. Mickey tiptoed back to her room and fell asleep almost before her head had reached the pillow.

Chapter
6

Mickey had a restless night, filled with
dreams of the smoke-filled bank, and she was
quite relieved when the blare of her alarm
clock finally sounded.

She rolled over and reached out clumsily,
knocking both the alarm and her battered
copy of *Cracking the Codes* off her bedside
table.

Mickey loved to read; whether that was finding out new pieces of information— like that wombats have cube-shaped poo— or getting lost in stories about exploring places under the sea or deep in the Amazon rainforest. Her favourite book of all was the memoirs of *Hildegarde L. McTavish*, spy extraordinaire, legendary codemaker, and Mickey's hero. She'd read *Cracking the Codes* so many times the spine had gone all wrinkly and some of the pages wouldn't lie flat any more.

Mickey had been researching real life spies when she first came across Hildegarde's memoirs. Although there were references to Hildegarde and her work as a spy in other places, Hildegarde herself had only ever written one book, years ago, and she hadn't been heard of since. Officially, Hildegarde was enjoying a peaceful retirement, but Mickey liked to think she still kept an eye out for a mystery to solve. Mickey often wondered what Hildegard would think of **COBRA**. She knew Hildegard had had a pet tortoise at one point but otherwise very few animals were mentioned in her book.

Hildegarde had been one of the country's top codemakers and famed for her logic and reasoning skills under pressure. Her speciality was code-cracking and she was known for creating imaginative and witty codes. Mickey loved the chapter where Hildegarde told the story of a spy long ago who had carried a secret message tattooed on his shaved head. His hair grew back, concealing the message, and it was only revealed when he went for a haircut and had his head shaved again.

Inspired by Hildegarde, Mickey had also experimented with creating her own invisible ink based around lemon juice which would only show up under certain conditions. Mickey spent more time than she would be willing to admit testing old receipts and shopping lists she found on the bus just in case they were messages from Hildegarde that had made their way out into the wild. Mickey hoped beyond hope that one day she could be as brave and clever as Hildegarde. She had even borrowed her surname to create her own spy alias, made by combining the name of your pet with the surname of someone you admire.

CREATING YOUR SPY ALIAS

Name of your pet + Surname of someone you admire

Mickey didn't have a pet so had borrowed Astrid's name instead as she had reasoned that the spider monkey wouldn't mind whereas Coby would probably find it mildly insulting. This meant that Mickey's secret spy name would be Astrid McTavish.

Mickey had some time before the **COBRA** meeting at 11 a.m. and was just settling down to reread the chapter about Hildegarde's invisible ink when she heard a tap at the window and looked up to see a sparrow perched on her windowsill. It nodded smartly at her then took flight leaving a note behind marked 'Mickey'.

Hoping it wasn't a summons to investigate more illegal mole activity Mickey retrieved the note and found herself faced with a code.

Mickey sighed. She loved Morse code and translating strings of numbers and letters into readable sentences but sometimes she struggled with visual codes. She spotted a small pawmark in the corner which she recognized as belonging to Astrid—of all the members of

COBRA Astrid was the one who seemed the most interested in codes and upon hearing about Mickey's difficulty with visual codes she had taken it upon herself to send Mickey a seemingly non-stop stream of different codes which she rather ominously said was to develop her skills for what may lie ahead.

This message looked as though it was written in spiral code. Mickey pinned it to the noticeboard above her desk, grabbed a notepad and pen and ran her eyes up and down and round the spiral. Spiral codes can be recognized as they look a bit like the charts opticians use to check your eyesight but the trick to solving them is to read them in a spiral starting in the top left corner.

As she slowly marked her way round the spiral with a pen she felt a grin spread across her face as she read the message, 'Hey Mickey, You solved it! Love From Astrid XX'

The secret to writing spiral codes is you need enough letters to fit neatly into a grid but if you don't have enough you can pad out the message by adding the number of 'X's you need at the end.

She was about to start trying to write back to Astrid in spiral code when she caught sight of her clock and realized it was time to head to the morning briefing at **COBRA**. She could tell by the shoes missing from the hall that her dad was already out at work so scribbled a quick note to her mum (who Mickey could tell was still sound asleep from the gentle snoring coming from her room) to let her know she would be back soon. She grabbed her jacket and set off—she couldn't wait to hear about Rupert's adventures and find out once and for all what the moles had been up to.

Chapter
7

Mickey's feet were used to pounding their way over to **COBRA** HQ by now, but she still felt a jolt of joy every time she ran down the path to 11 King Street—**COBRA** HQ. Number Eleven was set slightly back from the main road. There was an old battered shed which didn't look like much from the outside, or the inside really, but that was all part of the secret.

Mickey stepped into the shed which, as always, was empty apart from a goldfish swimming round and round in a tank that sat on an old table. Mickey bent down, made eye contact with the fish and slowly tapped her head three times—the **COBRA** Secret Agent greeting. The fish replied by blinking three times then gently tapped its head against the

bowl three times. A slow, creaking noise filled the room then the wall behind the goldfish fell away revealing the secret passageway to **COBRA** HQ.

Mickey scrambled through, nodded to Bertie who was standing behind his tall reception desk and made her way to the main meeting room where she ran into Astrid.

'Morning!' Mickey smiled. 'Thanks for my code, I solved it!'

'Well done!' said the monkey happily, reaching up to squeeze Mickey's hand with her paw. 'I'm glad, I really like spiral codes. My friend Maura introduced me to them years ago and said the trick to solving them is to visualize something round like the shell of a tortoise. And they're fun, sometimes we still write to each other using them!'

Mickey reached over to hold the door open. 'Thank you!' chirped Astrid. But as they entered the meeting room, Mickey could immediately tell that something was wrong.

Tilda was slowly fidgeting in her seat looking anxious, Clarke was sitting bolt upright and staring at the wall, and Coby was slithering around the floor in a figure of eight shape which was what she did when she was worried about something. Mickey quickly scanned the room and realized that Rupert— who usually prided himself on both his manners and his punctuality—was nowhere to be seen.

'Is Rupert not back yet?' Mickey asked, as she slid into her seat.

'Not yet,' said Tilda, her voice much more high-pitched than normal. 'We're quite worried about him.'

'He could just be running late,' said Clarke. 'Rupert is highly trained and knows what he's doing. He could come scurrying back in with the intel on the moles any minute now. We just have to sit and wait.'

'I hope you're right,' sighed Astrid.

As if on cue, there was a knock at the door, but it came from much higher up than Rupert could normally reach. It swung open and Bertie stuck his long neck into the room.

'A message has just arrived via Bird-Mail,'

he said. Astrid took the note, unfolded it and
read the message out loud:

DEAREST HIGH COMMITTEE,

I'M STILL ON THE TRAIL OF THE MOLES.
CAN'T COME IN NOW BUT I'LL BE BACK
FOR ONE OF MICKEY'S JAM SANDWICHES
SOON.

CHIN UP,
RUPERT

'Oh thank goodness,' said Tilda, sinking
her head down onto the table.

'At least he thought to send a note,' said
Clarke. 'I suppose we carry on with our other
lines of inquiry in the meantime.'

'Can I see the note?' asked Mickey
tentatively.

'Of course,' said Astrid passing it to her.
'It's nice that he misses your jam sandwiches!'

But Mickey didn't think this was nice.
Something felt wrong. *She* was the one who
liked jam sandwiches, Clarke liked fish paste,
Coby didn't eat bread, and Rupert always said
that filling sandwiches with jam was a missed
opportunity for cheese. He didn't like them
with jam so why had he said it in his note?
Mickey turned the letter over and over in
her hands while she thought, when suddenly
something caught her eye.

'OH!' she cried. 'There's something else—
look!'

'What is it?' asked Coby quickly, slithering
to Mickey's side.

'It could be nothing,' Mickey said, her brain

working quickly. 'BUT, there are some nibble marks down the side of the letter.' Mickey held the note up to the light for a better look. 'And if I'm not mistaken, these nibble marks spell out a recognized distress call—three short, three long, three short. That's Morse code for S.O.S.—it means he needs help.'

'They do look a bit like a code,' said Coby, tilting her head from side to side to get a better look.

'Also, Rupert really doesn't like jam sandwiches. It looks as though someone forced him to write this message but he has managed to leave us a couple of clues to let us know that he's in trouble,' said Mickey.

'Oh, clever Rupert!' said Astrid.

'But,' said Clarke, with a swish of his tail, 'if he needs help, who made him write the note—and where is he?'

Chapter

'That,' said Mickey, 'is what we need to find out.'

The High Committee were all looking anxiously around the room. It didn't feel right without Rupert, and Mickey couldn't help glancing over at his empty chair.

'Do you think the moles are holding him somewhere?' Tilda asked.

'That would fit with the timeline,' said Mickey.

'They have already made their first mistake by underestimating us,' said Coby. 'And we'll get Rupert back. Naturally, we'll all make this our top priority but Mickey, as Astrid and Clarke already have full workloads looking after the Domestic Animals and the International Animals I'd like you to take on Rupert's caseload and become Temporary Head of Wild Animals.'

'Mickey,' said Clarke, 'is not a wild animal.'

'Technically, I think humans *are*,' said Astrid.

'And,' said Tilda slowly, 'there is no rule that the head of any particular department has to be from that group of animals themselves.'

'Agreed,' said Coby. 'And as we all know there are some animals—snakes, for instance—who fit into all three categories—domestic, wild, and international. But there is no time to lose, we need to find out exactly what those moles were doing in the bank last night, and what happened to Rupert after he disappeared down that tunnel.'

'I think we should talk to Screech again,' said Mickey. 'He knows the bank better than any of us, so let's bring him in for questioning.'

'But it's daylight,' said Astrid. 'He won't be awake.'

'Then we wake him up,' said Coby bluntly.

'I'll go,' said Clarke with a gleam in his eye.

'He might be able to sleep through a note sent by Bird-Mail but he won't be able to sleep through *me*.'

Mickey nodded. Temporary Head of Wild Animals, she thought. She had no intention of messing it up but at the same time she could feel a knot forming in her stomach. So far the moles had had broken into a bank and now seemed to be holding Rupert captive. Who knew what else they were capable of?

She couldn't help but feel partly responsible for Rupert's disappearance as she'd been the last person to speak to him before he vanished. If she had done something differently, would Rupert be safe now?

However as she couldn't turn back time Mickey decided to channel her energy and frustrations into the one thing she knew she could do. Someone needed to find Rupert, work out what was going on with the moles, and put everything back to normal. Mickey knew that Hildegarde would have walked through fire to save her team, and Mickey was quite prepared to do just the same.

Chapter
9

Mickey was busy compiling a record of the previous evening's events when she heard the distinctive noise of Screech on the approach. Mickey opened the door and the owl shot through it then skidded all the way down the long gleaming table before coming to a stop right in front of Coby, who winced. Clarke trotted in quickly behind looking rather pleased with himself.

'Screech, we've saved you a seat,' said Astrid pointing out the visitor's chair. No one could quite bear to look at Rupert's empty seat.

'Thank you,' said Screech. He chose to perch on the back of the chair rather than sitting on it—even though that meant he kept having to spread his wings out in order to keep his balance and not to tip over the back of it and crash land on the floor. Then he opened his beak and let rip with a loud

'SCREEEEEEEEEECH'

'Screech, I've *told* you not to make that noise indoors,' said Clarke huffily.

'My sincerest apologies,' said Screech not sounding sincere or apologetic at all.

'Order!' called Coby. 'There will be no more screeching. This is a very urgent matter. One of our own is missing and we need all the information we can get.'

'Screech,' Mickey began, 'perhaps you could tell us what happened after we left last night. Did you or any of the other birds see anything that might give us more information about what the moles were doing?'

'Not really,' said the owl, tilting his head so he could scratch it with his foot.

'And what about this morning?'

'I don't really do mornings,' said the owl. 'I'm usually asleep then.'

'Aren't you curious about the goings on in the day?' asked Mickey.

'No,' said Screech. 'The only things that bother me are humans who wake me up with building work or shouting. It can be very disruptive.'

'But it's the daytime now, you must pay *some* attention?' probed Astrid.

'Nope,' said the owl. 'I'm only here now because Clarke arrived on the roof and batted me with his paw until I woke up and agreed to come.'

Clarke looked quite pleased with himself.

'You must know something Screech. I imagine that nothing gets past an observant and wise owl like you,' Mickey said.

Screech preened his feathers. 'Well . . . I have been seeing moles hanging around near the bank for a couple of weeks now. They never used to come near my patch—I assume it's some sort of territorial thing,' Screech explained. 'And there are more molehills than usual. I see a lot of those as I'm flying around. They're popping up all over town.'

'Interesting,' murmured Mickey.

'Animal activity is supposed to fly under the radar of the humans' attention, so they are risking a great deal by drawing attention to themselves,' said Coby. 'There was a mole that Rupert seemed to know in the bank— what was her name now—Fill something . . .'

'Phyllis?' asked Mickey, who was quite good with names.

'Yes. Now, normally I'd ask Rupert to try and find her—but that's a job for you now, Mickey.'

Mickey tried not to look overwhelmed.

'We should all help,' Astrid said quickly. 'Underground animals are hard to track down. Even Rupert struggled sometimes.'

'It's true,' drawled Clarke. 'They can't be reached by Bird-Mail, there's no easy route to get down there AND there are so many tunnels that are always being added to, you have no idea if you're going in the right direction.'

'That's right,' said Tilda. 'If you need to talk to an Underground Animal it is best if they come to you.'

'I suppose it must be quite hard to find a mole who does not want to be found,' pondered Mickey. 'Let's put out a call for a mole, any mole, to come in and explain themselves to us. Perhaps there is an innocent explanation for all of this?'

Coby nodded. 'A good plan. Tilda, could you please put out the call for the moles to come forward.'

'And Screech,' added Mickey turning to the owl, 'please could you ask the birds to keep a lookout from the skies and especially keep tabs on the bank.'

The owl nodded.

'Right,' said Mickey. 'I'll go and look for moles and molehills around the town. Let's get to work. We've got some moles to find, and a rat to rescue!'

Chapter

10

Finding moles who did not want to be found
proved to be even trickier than Mickey had
imagined. And yet she suddenly seemed
to be seeing molehills everywhere. As she
marched down King Street she only narrowly
avoided losing her footing as she tripped over
one. She was sure it hadn't been there when
she'd entered HQ earlier. Mickey scanned
her surroundings as she made her way home
and spotted another one in the middle of a
roundabout, another in the middle of a flower
bed, and even one on a tiny patch of grass
next to a lamp post that had caused the potted
plant that usually sat there to tilt at an odd
angle.

This reminded Mickey of the way the fire extinguisher had been lying on its side after the moles tunnelled into the bank. But while she could see evidence of their activity above ground, she had no idea what they were getting up to or how to find them underground. She tried calling down into their burrows but when no moles appeared she decided to head to the library and do some research. She marched into her local library and made a beeline for her favourite computer tucked away in the corner. Mickey logged in and began reading everything she could find about moles. Her investigation came along a lot faster once she'd removed the many articles about 'moles, skin condition' and instead focused on 'moles, animals'.

The bank incident had been the first time Mickey had seen a mole in real life which made sense as she read that they spent most of their time underground, were highly-skilled diggers (tunnelling up to 20 metres a day) and improved the quality of the soil by breaking it up, making it easier for plants to grow. Moles build tunnels with different rooms for sleeping and eating, and even stash earthworms in their 'larders' to eat later, biting off their heads so they can't escape.

But what had they been searching for in the bank?

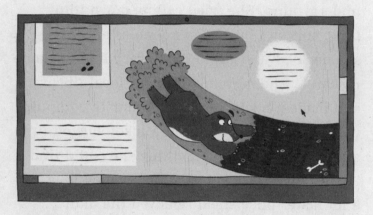

Money didn't seem like it would be much use to a mole, so Mickey ran a search for news articles about The United Bank. There were some about share prices and dividends which she didn't really understand but then she hit upon something interesting: the bank had recently announced a brand-new bank vault for only their richest customers. It was so exclusive that its exact location was a closely-guarded secret.

'An Impossible Vault,' Mickey exhaled, delighted with her discovery. This, she realized, was exactly why a Human Liaison Officer was so important for **COBRA**. Rupert may have an advantage with wild animals, but she had an advantage with humans, and she was fairly sure she was the only one who read the human newspapers. 'Too depressing,' Astrid had said when she'd brought one in once; 'Too big for my paws,' had been Rupert's take; 'Not enough about cats,' Clarke had said.

Mickey kept searching and read about how the bank were targeting billionaires to bank with them and use The Impossible Vault, and it was said to be the most expensive storage facility in the country. Mickey wasn't sure what a billionaire might be storing that would be of interest to a mole. As she couldn't find any moles to question she couldn't know for sure but it seemed likely that the moles might have been looking for the location of The Impossible Vault. And if they were willing to break into The United Bank and also hold Rupert captive, it seemed as though they were willing to go to any lengths to get inside. They had to be stopped!

Chapter

11

Mickey presented her
theory at **COBRA** HQ
first thing the next
morning.

'You think the moles are looking for this Impossible Vault?' asked Coby, studying a printout of the article that Mickey had brought with her.

'I think so,' Mickey replied. 'It would explain why they broke into the bank and why there are molehills popping up everywhere. If Rupert was onto them, perhaps they decided to hold him captive until they've completed their mission?'

'It does look as though Mickey might be onto something,' Tilda said slowly.

'They were searching for something in the bank,' Mickey continued, 'and I think they must be looking for clues or even the vault itself. That must be why Screech has been noticing more mole activity around the bank. But we won't know for sure until we speak to a mole—has anyone made contact with a mole?'

'Not yet,' said Coby. 'Curiously none of the moles have responded to our request to come in and talk to us so we are escalating that to a direct order. In the meantime, why don't you and Astrid go and investigate at The United Bank and see if you can find out any more about this so-called Impossible Vault?'

'And we'll step up the search for a mole, any mole. And bring them in for . . . a friendly chat', said Clarke, narrowing his eyes and licking his lips.

'Good plan,' said Astrid, 'though you better not try to eat the witnesses. Again.'

Mickey and Astrid had been out on fieldwork duties before, and had learned that the best way for a small girl and a spider monkey to be together in public without causing any alarm was for Astrid to perch on Mickey's back and loop her long limbs around her arms so that any casual passer-by would think she was some form of novelty backpack.

They both had to be careful when talking to each other, so they kept their voices low, and if anyone did overhear either of them they probably assumed Mickey was just talking on a hands-free phone call. Sometimes tech could be useful even when you weren't actually using it.

The autumn weather had turned cooler and Mickey felt even more of a chill as they stepped into the bank's airy main hall. She made a beeline for a seat in the waiting area and sat down. She took out her phone hoping she looked like a bored kid waiting patiently for a parent, but actually her brain was scanning the room looking for anything that might be helpful. The fire extinguisher now standing firmly upright made her wonder how many tunnels the moles had dug under the floorboards. The room had high ceilings with elegant decorated columns dotted around and cold blue walls. There was a soft hum of conversation, occasionally punctured by people in the lengthy queue at the desk complaining to each other about how long they had been waiting.

'And is The Impossible Vault open for business now?' she heard a smartly-dressed woman asking a bank cashier.

'Oh yes. I'd be happy to give you some more

information,' replied a bank worker. 'Please follow me through to our private banking suite.'

This was it! Mickey sprang to her feet, backpack in tow, and followed them. They were heading towards the door marked 'PRIVATE' that the moles had tried to get through when they set off the alarm. The customer politely held the door open for Mickey and she shot through triumphantly. The smartly-dressed woman and the bank cashier made their way through another door, leaving Mickey in another reception room.

'Can I help you?' asked a red-haired receptionist sitting at a long shiny desk. 'Are you looking for someone?'

'Yes,' said Mickey, thinking quickly, 'the person who just went into the office was my mum. She said to wait here while she asked some questions about your new vault?'

'Very well.' The receptionist lost interest and waved her hand in the direction of the luxury leather armchairs that made up the waiting area. They were much nicer than the

plastic seats in the main foyer.

'What do you think?' Mickey murmured to her backpack.

'I don't think this is the sort of place that usually admits spider monkeys,' Astrid whispered back.

Suddenly a tall, well-dressed elderly gentleman was ushered through the door by a clerk in a bank uniform and the receptionist's attention was diverted. The man had a fine grey moustache and was wearing a smart but old green tweed jacket. One hand was gripping a walking stick and the other was carrying a brand-new leather briefcase. Mickey took the opportunity to find the best seat for listening to see if she could gather any more information and watched as the receptionist stood up to greet him.

'I was just explaining to this gentleman that of course, we can't tell anyone the real location of The Impossible Vault,' the bank clerk said to her.

'I must say, I find the idea of entrusting my most precious items to you and then not knowing where they are being held, rather alarming,' the gentleman replied.

'Perhaps you'd like to make an appointment with one of our banking consultants and they can reassure you that your precious items really are in safe hands,' the bank clerk smiled. 'Felicia is currently talking to another potential client but if we can just make you an appointment she'll be able to explain everything in more detail.'

The older gentleman rested his bag on the desk then took out a gold pocket watch and frowned at it. 'I rather think I am running out of time—perhaps I could come back on Wednesday afternoon. Should I bring the items with me?'

'Not at first. Felicia will talk you through it all as well as our various payment tiers sir,' said the bank clerk, keen to make that booking.

'But if time were of the essence, how quickly could my items arrive in the vault?'

'The same day, sir, don't worry. The United Bank is of course a safe place for your belongings, but concierge service is included, and particularly valuable items will be couriered directly to The Impossible Vault, from this building,' the receptionist added.

The elderly man seemed to be losing interest, so the bank clerk started throwing in more details. Mickey realized this woman was *very* keen that he choose to use The Impossible Vault, and wondered if she was working on commission. At the same time, the gentleman seemed to be trying to get as much information as possible without agreeing to pay to store his goods in the vault. Mickey imagined such a service would not be cheap. She kept watching to see who would cave first.

'You see,' the receptionist continued, 'this vault is not just protected by security measures like cameras and locks. What if I told you that it contains not one, not two but three top-secret rooms of encryption and was developed by one of this country's top code-crackers.'

Mickey nudged Astrid with excitement.

She wondered what sort of protection a code-cracker would put on a vault! The gentleman seemed intrigued too. His whole face lit up and for a minute he looked years younger.

'Can I take a name and telephone number please, sir?' she continued, looking up to type in the details as one of the bank's security guards came marching down the corridor towards them.

'Yes of course,' said the man, though Mickey thought he seemed slightly flustered. 'It's Frederick . . . Frederick Newton.'

Unfortunately for Mickey her detecting ended right there as while the guard had looked approvingly at Mr Newton, he looked *very* suspiciously at her.

'What are you doing there?' he asked briskly. 'Children shouldn't be in the banking suite.'

'I'm just waiting for my mum. She's in one of the meeting rooms, discussing The Impossible Vault.'

The guard's face relaxed and he smiled at her. 'Very well, do you know which one?'

Mickey was about to point to the room the smartly-dressed woman had entered but then saw the door open as she stepped out into the corridor.

'Ah, actually, I'll wait for her in the main hall,' Mickey said quickly, realizing she needed to scarper before the receptionist asked her to collect her 'daughter'. 'Thank you for letting me wait here,' she gabbled as she grabbed hold of Astrid's paws. 'Goodbye!'

Mickey tried to get a better look at Mr Newton as she left but he was deeply engrossed in some paperwork. She wondered if he really was trying to put something in the vault and if so, what could it be?

Chapter

All the details Mickey and Astrid had managed to acquire were blown out of the water when they arrived back at the **COBRA** meeting room to hear that Screech's air patrol had managed to locate a mole.

'One of the seagulls found him digging near the fountains in the city square and managed to nab him,' Screech was reporting as they raced in. 'Should be along shortly.'

'Ooff, get off,' they heard from the corridor. Bertie the giraffe appeared looking stern, accompanying two seagulls who were flying down the corridor while holding a furious looking mole in a temporary cage made of their clawed feet. The mole's velvety fur was all messed up and pointing in different directions, as if there had been a struggle.

Mickey jumped to dim the lights in case that helped as the mole was clearly

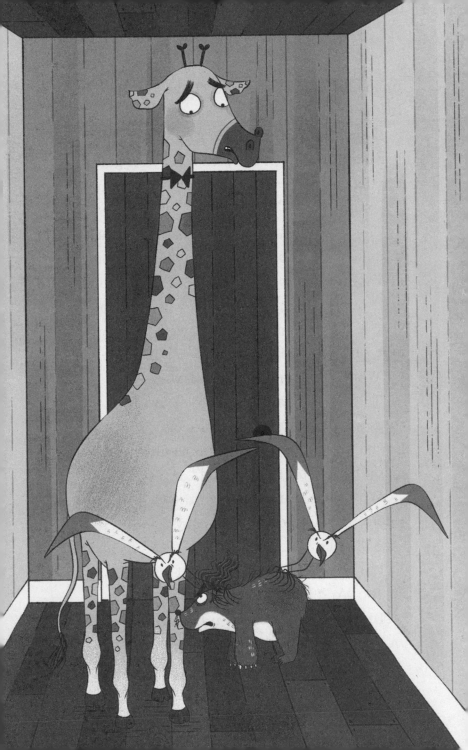

uncomfortable being both above ground and inside a building.

'Excellent work,' hissed Coby. 'You can leave him here. Bertie, please stay on guard in the doorway in case our visitor tries to make an escape before we're done . . . catching up.'

The seagulls dropped the mole onto the middle of the table, then squawked a goodbye and soared out of the room. Bertie closed the door behind them, checked it was completely secure then stood in the doorway, blocking the exit with his sizeable frame.

'What's your name?' asked Mickey.

'T . . . Troy,' said the mole. 'But there's no need for all this security, I'm happy to talk to you, this is all just a big misunderstanding.'

'Why were you digging in the city square in the middle of the day?' asked Mickey.

'I'm a mole,' said Troy. 'That's what we do for fun. And for work.'

'Did your work take you to The United Bank on Friday night?' asked Coby.

'Not mine, that was the others . . .' the mole began to say then realized he'd just incriminated other moles and seemed to clam up.

'Who?' asked Clarke quickly. 'We know moles were there, you were seen.'

'Maybe . . . maybe some of my friends just got a bit high-spirited?' said Troy.

'I have never been so high-spirited I *broke into a bank*,' said Coby fiercely. The mole jumped.

'And,' added Mickey, 'if only some of the moles were involved why did all of you ignore the **COBRA** request to come and talk to us?'

Troy looked momentarily panicked. 'We were . . . all busy?' he tried.

Coby slithered forward and drew her head down until she had direct eye contact with the mole. 'Tell me what is going on,' she hissed.

The mole shook again. 'I don't know! Really, I don't! But some of the more high-spirited moles were talking about another gathering. Tonight at 7 p.m. by the docks. But that's all I know.'

'Hey! Look over there—more moles!'
Troy cried. The members of **COBRA** fell for
the oldest trick in the book. As they briefly
glanced around, Troy took his chance and
scuttled through Bertie's feet and made a
dash for the corridor and to freedom. Bertie
turned to run after him, but it was no use.
The mole was gone.

Astrid turned to the rest of the High
Committee.

'Do you think he's telling the truth?'

'It's hard to tell,' said Mickey.

'Aren't moles quite untrustworthy—that's
why your human word 'mole' means someone
who betrays people,' said Clarke.

'You can't say that!' Mickey gasped. 'That
would be like saying all cats are vain and . . .'
she thought better of finishing that sentence
and trailed off. Clarke already looked furious.

'Let's do another search for moles who
might be willing to talk to us. Everyone check
in with your contacts then we'll stake out the
docks at 7 p.m. If those moles are plotting
something, we'll be ready for them.'

Chapter
13

Mickey had some time before the
stakeout, so she went outside to think.
She climbed the big tree outside
and as she perched on her favourite
branch she heard a rustling above her
and a small robin appeared on the

branch next her. It looked her straight in the eye and tapped its head three times with its wing. Mickey looked straight into its beady eyes and blinked three times. The official COBRA greeting.

'Mickey?' the robin tweeted in a soft sing-song voice.

'Yes,' she replied.

'I have something for you,' it chirruped. The tiny bird ruffled its feathers and dropped a small, tightly-rolled scroll of paper in front of her. Then it turned and flew off before Mickey had a chance to ask any follow-up questions. She quickly unravelled the message and found herself faced with a blank sheet of paper. Just as her brain started to whirr with thoughts of invisible ink and the best way to reveal the message she realized there was one much easier option to try first. She turned the paper over and found she had simply been looking at the wrong side. The other was covered in what was—thank goodness—Rupert's neat handwriting. The seemingly random selection of letters looked like a code—much more her thing. She looked at it and frowned.

TREPUR
.YRRUH ESAELP DNA RAED
YM KCUL FO TSEB .M.P.5 TA
GNINEVE SIHT YNAPMOC
GNIRETAC ENAL NEERG EHT
TA UOY TEEM OT DEERGA
SAH EHS. NIBOR GNISSAP A OT
ETON SIHT SSAP OT DEERGA
DNA EM GNIPLEH NEEB SAH
SILLYHP TUB MA I EREHW
WONK T'NOD I DIARFA M'I
.SREHTO EHT NRAW .EREHT OG
TON TSUM UOY .SKCOD EHT
OT GNIOG OTNI UOY KCIRT
OT YRT NEHT ESOPRUP NO
DERUTPAC EB OT MIH ROF SI
NALP RIEHT. YORT TSURT TON
OD. KNAB EHT TA NI-KAERB
EHT RETFA MEHT DEWOLLOF
I NEHW EM DEPPANDIK DNA
DEHSUBMA OHW SELOM EHT
YB DNUORGREDNU DLEH
GNIEB MA I ,RAED YM

Perhaps it was because her brain was working super-fast to try to deal with the current mission—or because her eyes spotted the paw mark at the top of the code when usually you signed a letter at the end of the message—but Mickey very quickly realized this message may have looked confusing but it was actually written in backwards code. To solve it all she had to do was start at the end and spell out each words. Working speedily she translated the message:

MY DEAR, I AM BEING HELD UNDERGROUND BY THE MOLES WHO AMBUSHED AND KIDNAPPED ME WHEN I FOLLOWED THEM AFTER THE BREAK–IN AT THE BANK. DO NOT TRUST TROY. THEIR PLAN IS FOR HIM TO BE CAPTURED ON PURPOSE THEN TRY TO TRICK YOU INTO GOING TO THE DOCKS. YOU MUST NOT GO THERE. WARN THE OTHERS. I'M AFRAID I DON'T KNOW WHERE I AM BUT PHYLLIS HAS BEEN HELPING ME AND AGREED TO PASS THIS NOTE TO A PASSING ROBIN. SHE HAS AGREED TO MEET YOU AT THE GREEN LANE CATERING COMPANY THIS EVENING AT 5 P.M. BEST OF LUCK MY DEAR AND PLEASE HURRY. RUPERT

Her heart was thumping as she read the whole message. Rupert was alive, and being held by the moles somewhere underground. And he'd managed to warn them, just in time, as Coby was right this minute planning the group excursion to the docks. She had to warn them.

'Stop!!!' Mickey cried as she ran back inside, where she found Clarke and Coby sitting with their heads close together.

'Look!' she cried, brandishing the letter. 'It's another note from Rupert—the docks are a trap!'

'What?' said Coby sharply, taking the letter with her tail and looking at Mickey's translation.

'I knew that mole couldn't be trusted,' said Clarke.

'We must act quickly,' said Coby. 'I'll call in the others—no one is to go to the docks.'

'And I'll investigate the Green Lane Catering Company in case Phyllis is there,' said Mickey. 'We need to act fast. Are you coming Clarke?'

But Clarke had already sprung to his paws and was ready for action.

'Let's go!' he said.

Mickey and Clarke trotted through the city's streets, keeping to the shadows. Mickey felt as though she could catch soft movements in the gloom but when she turned her head to look more closely they were gone. It felt as though the moles were literally running rings around **COBRA**, but finally they seemed to have a lead.

Even though they were walking as fast as they could without attracting suspicion, it was a cold evening, and Mickey rubbed her hands together to try and generate some extra warmth. She was glad when they turned the corner onto Green Lane. The front door of the catering company was covered in posters for a local funfair and the building seemed deserted. Mickey tried the door, but it was locked.

She walked around the rest of the building, Clarke running ahead of her, and realized there was quite a large outdoor yard blocked off by a wall.

'I'll go first,' whispered Clarke, head turned towards a wall so no one would see his mouth moving. 'Lost cat.'

'Lost cat' was a tactic Mickey and Clarke had realized would allow them into almost any location. There were very few people who would stop a young girl retrieving her beloved cat.

Clarke sprang up onto the wall outside the Green Lane Catering Company then yowled pitifully as he toppled over onto the other side.

'MR MOGINGTON!' cried Mickey, for the sake of anyone watching, though she'd looked around first and was fairly sure the coast was clear. Quickly she scrambled over the wall herself and found herself in the yard at the back of the building. The yard was full of weeds that had gone to seed, with wooden pallets, an upturned wheelbarrow, and several industrial-sized tins of tomatoes waiting to be recycled scattered around the space.

'It's very messy,' said Clarke wrinkling his nose. 'And I don't see anyone here.'

But Mickey was not an experienced codebreaker for nothing. Scanning the yard she noticed a line of dry molehills which suggested they had been there a while. They looked very different from the freshly turned molehill next to the wheelbarrow. Mickey knelt down to have a closer look.

'Phyllis?' she whispered. 'It's Mickey. Are you here?'

A very faint knock came from inside the wheelbarrow.

'Clarke! Over here,' said Mickey, slightly wary in case it was a trap. She watched Clarke take up a position next to her, paws ready in case whoever was under the barrow should attack or try to flee.

'On three,' she whispered. 'One . . . two . . . three!'

She tipped the wheelbarrow onto its side, groaning slightly under its weight and Clarke sprang forwards and placed his paws around

the mole who was now staring straight up at them, and looked it straight in the eye.

'Who are you?' he asked firmly.

'Ph-Ph-Phyllis!' said the mole as she wriggled around and tried to cover her eyes. 'I'm a friend of Rupert's. But it's not safe to talk here.'

And she refused to say another word.

Chapter

14

'What do you mean she won't speak?' said
Astrid curiously when Mickey and Clarke
arrived back at the meeting room. They had
left Phyllis in the care of Bertie who was
determined not to be outsmarted by a mole
twice in the same day.

'Exactly that,' said Clarke. 'But after
Troy's stunt with the docks we need to be

extra careful. This could be another trap so anything she does say will be taken with a large pinch of salt in case she is also trying to trick us.'

'Rupert's note said that she was helping him,' Mickey explained. 'And she came with us. I think she's scared about someone overhearing her.'

'Well we can take care of that,' said Coby. 'Bring her in.'

As Temporary Head of Wild Animals Mickey took charge and brought Phyllis into the room. The mole was so nervous she was shaking.

'You don't have to do this if you don't want to,' Mickey said gently.

'I do,' said Phyllis, giving herself one last big shake all over and then scuttled towards the table, guided by Mickey.

'Take a seat,' said Clarke, baring his teeth as he pointed to the visitor's chair with his tail.

'Welcome Phyllisssss, we hope you have

some answers for us.' said Coby, rearing her head up and looking down at the mole who was tucked into the furthest back corner of her chair, but she met Coby's gaze then leaned forward and stood up strongly on her two back feet.

'Are there any moles here?' she asked urgently.

'Yes,' said Tilda. '*You're* here.'

'Phyllis,' Mickey continued, 'it's just us and this is a safe place to talk, I promise. The moles seem to have been ignoring direct **COBRA** orders to come in and talk to us and Troy scarpered as soon as he told us about the meeting at the docks. What's going on Phyllis? This seems out of character for moles. Is someone else giving them orders?' Mickey knew this was a shot in the dark but suddenly, it seemed to make sense.

Phyllis gave a nod, so small if you blinked you'd have missed it.

'Do you know who it is?'

Another tiny nod. 'Yes, but you're not going to like it.' She hesitated.

'Phyllisssss,' hissed Coby, puffing out the hood around her neck in annoyance. 'One of our best agents is missing, we still don't have a *ssatisssfactory* explanation for The United Bank break-in *and* there are molehills all over town. There are many things I don't like, but what I really don't like is when *molesss* disobey direct *instructio^{nsss}* for help or when they *wasssste* my time.'

Coby looked like she could go on for a while so Mickey cut in.

'Please Phyllis,' Mickey said. 'We know Rupert's your friend. He's ours too. He wouldn't hurt a soul AND WE NEED TO FIND HIM. If there's anything that can help us find him please tell us.'

'Rupert was being held in one of our tunnels. I know because he gave me the note for you. But when I went back there, he was gone. The moles move him around all the time, precisely to make it harder to track him down. Oh, this has all got so terribly out of paw.'

'If you want Rupert back safely, as we do,

then you must tell us who is behind all this,'
Mickey said.

The mole looked down at the floor,
hesitated and then lifted her head boldly
and addressed the room. 'It's Harry. Your
old Human Liaison Officer. And *your*
predecessor,' she said, nodding at Mickey.
'He's making the moles look for The
Impossible Vault. He wants to get inside and
steal the precious treasure there.'

'Oh *great,'* she heard Clarke mutter behind
them.

'Surely not,' hissed Coby. 'We told him to
stay out of town.'

'The Impossible Vault may have been
enough to lure him back,' said Astrid.

'Right,' said Mickey. 'But why are the moles
helping him?'

'Well,' Phyllis said, then buried her face
in her hands. 'I'm sorry, please don't take
this the wrong way but, well, some of the
moles feel that we're constantly overlooked,
being underground creatures. Everything
happens above ground; all your meetings are

above ground and we always have to come to you. No one ever comes down to see us. Harry turned up telling us he'd heard of this spectacular new underground HQ for us. One that was so secure it would make **COBRA** HQ look like a toy. And he said he would help us to find it as its location was a closely-guarded secret.'

'And this HQ is The Impossible Vault?' asked Mickey.

Phyllis nodded. 'That's what he called it. He said we shouldn't let on to **COBRA** because you'd try to claim it for yourselves but that it would be a natural fit for us. He even offered to clear out the human junk, so we would have the most space possible.'

'*Very* generous of him, offering to take away all those jewels and treasures,' said Clarke dryly.

'We were all forbidden from saying anything. He's got all the moles on his side and is feeding them information and worms, so they trust him and can always be one step ahead of you. That's where Troy's capture and the message about the docks came from. Harry saw Mickey and Astrid at the bank when he was investigating and knew you were on his trail. He set up the trick at the docks, planning to get rid of you once and for all.'

Mickey gasped. 'Oh, I knew that man looked familiar!' she cried, suddenly placing him. 'He was in disguise as Mr Frederick Newton.'

'Oh funny,' said Tilda, remembering. 'Fred was the name of his first pet—Fred the Dalmatian.'

Mickey could have kicked herself. This was the classic 'work out your spy name' trick and she'd missed it!

NAME OF YOUR PET +
SURNAME OF SOMEONE
YOU ADMIRE =
YOUR SPY NAME

'So what happens next?' asked Coby. 'I presume the molehills that are 'decorating' this town are attempts to locate The Impossible Vault?'

'Yes,' said Phyllis, 'he's got the moles searching, but so far no one has had any luck. I am ashamed to say that I, too, was on Harry's side, until I saw how he treated Rupert. Maybe I could try to get more moles on your side? Not all of them even know what has happened to Rupert.'

'If Rupert is underground then the moles are our best chance of finding him,' said Mickey. 'You're the experts at life underground! Do you really think you can get more to help you?'

'Yes, I think so,' replied Phyllis. 'Give me 24 hours, and I'll try to come back with either Rupert or a troop of moles willing to step up the search for him.'

'Are you really going to let her leave?' Clarke asked. 'She's the only link to the moles we have. Wouldn't it be more interesting to hold her captive and send a ransom note of our own.'

Phyllis began to tremble.

'Clarke!' Mickey cried. 'You know that's not how we do things in **COBRA**. When others go low, we go high. I think Phyllis is our best bet to find Rupert. We're going to need to trust her and I do.'

'Thank you, I won't let you down,' said Phyllis as she turned and scampered out of the room.

'I certainly hope you can trust her,' said Clarke. 'Otherwise you've just let our best lead walk out of here. If you've got this wrong it won't just be the mission in trouble but Rupert's life.'

Chapter
15

It was a very dispirited Mickey who walked through the main door to her building later that evening. Coby had said there was nothing else that could be done that evening but Screech and the birds had been briefed to keep searching above ground while Phyllis tried to gather moles to help search below ground. She felt a nervous tumbling feeling that ran through her whole body. They needed to get this right, stop Harry, and bring Rupert back safely. That was a lot of work for the Temporary Head of Wild Animals, but she was determined to see that it was done.

She was expecting the flat to be quiet when she got home so she was planning a solid hour of heavy thinking, but she was surprised by both of her parents who appeared in the hall as she pushed open the front door.

'You're back late! How was the library?'

asked her mum.

'Er . . . good, thanks,' said Mickey, hoping
they wouldn't find out that she'd actually
been exploring an abandoned building and
questioning a mole. 'I thought you were
working tonight?' said Mickey.

'I was supposed to be, but we haven't sat
down together for so long I thought I'd take
the evening off.'

'Yes, we've both been rather snowed under
lately, but we don't want you to feel left out,'
her dad added.

'Exactly,' said her mum. 'We're always
here if you need us and we thought perhaps
tonight we might order food from the Italian
place round the corner?'

'With garlic bread?' asked Mickey, feeling
her stomach rumble.

'Definitely with garlic bread,' said
her dad, smiling. Mickey looked at their
happy, expectant faces and decided her
planning could wait. She was hungry, and
it was important for secret agents to be
well-fuelled. Hildegarde often said,

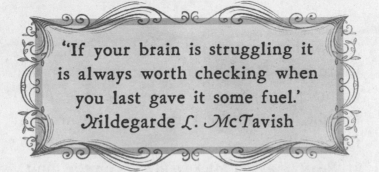

Mickey decided this was excellent advice to take. Especially when there was garlic bread on offer.

They didn't even need to look at the menu as they always ordered the same thing, then they sat around the kitchen table solving that day's puzzles in the newspaper until the food arrived. Mickey munched her way happily through a Margherita pizza while her parents had a seafood linguine dish to share. Then there was strawberry ice cream for pudding and Mickey's heart soon felt as full as her stomach.

'What do you want to do for the rest of the evening?' asked her dad as he scraped the last bit out of his bowl with a spoon.

'I was going to read Hildegarde's memoirs again,' Mickey said, hoping she might find some inspiration to help crack the case in there.

'Oh, that reminds me,' said her mum. 'I heard from James at work that there's a new documentary about the security services on tonight. They've discovered some new archive footage.'

'Really?' asked Mickey, always on the hunt for more Hildegarde inspiration and hoping this could give her the spark she needed to fit the pieces of the puzzle together.

'Yes, it's archive footage, with stories from some real spies, though they'll have to blur out their faces of course.'

'That makes sense,' agreed Mickey, intrigued.

'Shall we give it a go?' her mum asked.

She didn't need to wait for an answer as Mickey was already buzzing with anticipation and settling down in front of the TV.

Mickey watched as the screen filled with tales of mystery and daring. Even though Coby had said there was nothing else she could do tonight she couldn't stop thinking about Rupert. Her brain was still turning over ideas but as she kept watching, one of

the stories drew her attention completely. The camera introduced a disguised agent and Mickey sat up in her seat. She was sure this was Hildegarde. Mickey was so used to reading her writing that she was sure she recognized her turns of phrase. And there was another clue: this agent was also wearing a small tortoise badge on her lapel.

This was the closest Mickey had come to seeing her hero talk in person and she leaned forward intently. The programme switched back to the main presenter:

THIS AGENT WAS RESPONSIBLE FOR DREAMING UP THE MOST SECURE VAULT THE WORLD HAD EVER SEEN. THE IMPOSSIBLE VAULT WOULD CONTAIN THREE ROOMS FULL OF ENCRYPTION PUZZLES GIVING IT UNPRECEDENTED LEVELS OF PROTECTION FROM ANY PERSON WHO MIGHT TRY TO ILLEGALLY GAIN ACCESS.

Three rooms? thought Mickey. The Impossible Vault? It *had* to be the same one. The man at the bank had said The Impossible Vault was designed by the country's top minds and you didn't get brighter than 𝒳ildegarde 𝓛. 𝒨cTavish. Perhaps, the code only seemed impossible if you were thinking about it in the wrong way. People who didn't know Hildegarde's workings might think it was impossible to crack but Mickey had been studying her work for years!

The documentary then switched to footage of the blurry agent in her garden.

'Oh sorry, let me just move Maura out of the way.' She leaned down and carefully relocated an elderly-looking tortoise. 'Sorry about that, she's so inquisitive.'

Maura, thought Mickey. She was sure she'd heard that name somewhere recently. She was sure it wasn't someone's spy code name this time, but she couldn't remember where it had come up.

'I just find people don't stop to smell the flowers often enough,' Hildegarde said, her voice slightly robotic as it had been disguised. 'But they're so useful—in my garden I have lavender to help me sleep, rosemary for memory, and mint to aid digestion.'

Mickey's mind was consumed by The Impossible Vault. If it was part of Hildegarde's legacy, then Mickey might be able to figure out the location of the vault. Finding the vault might be a way to find Harry and force him to return Rupert. For the first time that evening she felt a glimmer of hope. Perhaps now was the time to utilize all her Hildegarde knowledge. The other members of **COBRA** didn't know much about Hildegarde, but Mickey was a world-class expert!

Chapter

16

'And you really think The Impossible Vault
was designed by this Hildegrade?' asked
Clarke curiously, when Mickey related her
theory at **COBRA** HQ.

'Hilde*garde*!' corrected Mickey. *'She* was one of the country's top spies! She's my codebreaking hero! If she's behind the vault that would explain why it's supposed to be so impossible to break into. The person at the bank said it had three rooms of encryption.'

'And we think Harry plans to get past all three?' queried Tilda.

'Yes,' said Mickey. 'I don't think he'd be able to do it on his own. But . . . he has the moles helping him and as they're experts in both digging and All Things Underground I think there's a chance they might be able to do it. We just need to find the vault before they do.'

'It might be worth trying . . .' began Tilda when she was suddenly drowned out by some very loud banging.

Mickey sprang to her feet to investigate, dashing to the entrance closely followed by the rest of the High Committee. She found the goldfish swimming round and round its bowl and Bertie the giraffe putting all his weight against the door to the shed while his legs were stretched out covering parts of the floor which seemed to be rippling in places as if there were something underneath.

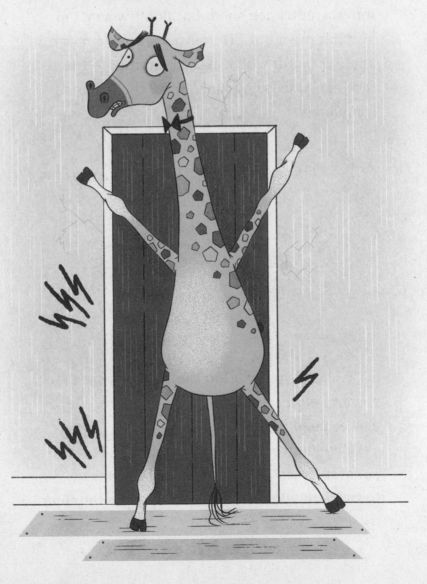

'Bertie!' cried Mickey. 'Are you okay?
What's happening?'

'It seems some moles are trying to burrow
into the entrance shed, but don't worry I'm
keeping them out.' He moved a foot to cover
another plank which was beginning to tilt and
threatened to be pushed out of the ground
completely.

'Tilda, if you wouldn't mind covering that
corner, and Clarke the one over there?' Bertie
asked, nodding with his head.

Coby glanced round to check the secret
panel into the HQ was sealed then moved
towards the door and hissed towards the floor.

'What do you think you are doing? If you wish to pay a visit use the usual channels.'

The noise stopped, and the floor went still.

'Have they . . . gone?' asked Mickey.

Everyone listened carefully and heard a slippery sound like someone going down a slide, followed by some more digging and shuffling. And then there was a low tap on the door.

'Yes?' said Bertie, dipping his head down to speak through the crack at the bottom.

'Sorry about that, we were aiming for just outside, not just under your headquarters. Can we come in?'

Bertie turned to the group. 'There seems to be a group of moles outside,' he whispered.

'I see,' said Coby. 'MOLESSSS!' she hissed. 'Stand back! I do not trust you to enter my headquarters, so we will meet you outside.'

Coby led the way, followed by Mickey, Tilda, Clarke, and Astrid.

Just to the side of the shed's door was a group of half a dozen moles, all wearing sunglasses. The one at the front stepped forward.

'Hello,' he said,
'I'm Troy. We have
already met.'

Mickey heard Clarke growl in warning.
Troy was the mole who had delivered the fake
message about the docks.

'What do you think you are doing?'
thundered Coby. 'This is an absolute breach
of our rules. How dare you try to tunnel into
our headquarters.'

'Have you changed your mind? Are you
here to help us?' asked Astrid hopefully.

'No,' said Troy, flatly, 'I'm here to issue our
demands.'

'WHAT?' said Mickey.

'We took Rupert when he tried to follow

us out of the bank, and when we realized you were looking for him we moved him again, sharpish. Harry says he'll give you Rupert if you give him something in exchange.'

'We don't give in to bribes . . .' hissed Coby.

Troy ignored her and carried on. 'As you've probably worked out by now, the moles *are* working with Harry, trying to locate The Impossible Vault. However, it is taking too long and now he would like **COBRA** to help us look.'

'Which will never happen!' spat Coby furiously.

'That's what he said you would say,' said Troy, rocking back and forth on his hind legs. 'But he has Rupert. And we know *how* to get into The Impossible Vault—even if we can't find it. Thanks to his recent visit to the bank, Harry has given a very special box to the bank to deposit inside the vault. And the box just happens to have Rupert inside.'

'No!' gasped Astrid.

'Yes! Harry knows Mickey and Astrid saw him at the bank when he was making enquiries,' the mole added. 'He went back to the bank and deposited his 'valuables', but the thing is . . . there isn't very much oxygen in the metal case he's being held inside. So if I were you I'd get a move on. And in case you're thinking of not cooperating he sent this to help you make your mind up.'

One of the other moles scuttled forward and passed something to Troy who then turned and presented it to Mickey.

'A stopwatch?' she said, turning it over in her hands. '4 hours, 35 minutes, and 56 seconds,' she read aloud. 'Now 55 seconds, 54, 53 . . . What is it counting down to?'

'That's how long Rupert has left before he runs out of oxygen. Good luck.' said Troy with a smug smile. Then the group of moles turned and fled back down their recently-dug hole.

'Why you little . . .' began Clarke, as he jumped towards him and batted the air where Troy had stood, but it was no use. The moles were gone.

'Weren't we trying to *stop* anyone breaking into The Impossible Vault,' asked Tilda slowly.

'*Yesss*,' said Coby. 'But we have to do it. Rupert's life is at risk!'

Chapter 17

The members of **COBRA** were back in HQ, standing in stunned silence. Mickey, gripping the digital stop watch, was painfully aware of each second that ticked by. She knew they had to be fast.

'What we need . . . is Phyllis, has anyone heard from her?'

Tilda, Clarke, Astrid, and Coby all shook their heads.

'I knew we shouldn't have trusted that

stupid mole,' said Clarke.

'Oh really?' asked Bertie, stretching his long neck into the room. 'I have Phyllis at reception and she's . . . well she's brought some friends.'

'Let them in!' Mickey cried. Her timing could not have been better.

Phyllis came tentatively into the room.

'We heard what Troy's done. We're so sorry and we're here to help. Come on team!'

Dozens of moles came pouring into the room to join her. Some climbed into the vacant visitors' seats though nobody sat in Rupert's chair. Astrid and Tilda moved to one side of their seats so more moles could fit around the table. One particularly bold mole tried to share with Clarke but thought the better of it and climbed back down quick sharp. The moles who couldn't get seats lined up in a neat row.

'Phyllis!' said Mickey, 'this is quite a lot of moles.'

'We feel terrible for what has happened,' Phyllis began. 'We were all taken in by

Harry's promise of a new underground headquarters. He promised us that taking Rupert was just a temporary measure and that we would let him go as soon as we had found our new headquarters, but then obviously some of us felt uneasy about it, and then upon hearing that Harry has put Rupert in the vault, well, we want this to stop and we're here to help.'

Mickey smiled. With their own gang of moles and the combined powers of **COBRA**, they might be able to beat Harry, Troy, and *their* moles, and have a real chance of saving the day!

'Unfortunately, Troy and his gang are not to be trusted but Harry's lost the backing of the majority of moles,' said Phyllis, 'and Rowan has some news that may help us.'

One of the moles sharing a seat with Tilda stood up.

'Yes, it's just something I spotted. It might be nothing but I was tunnelling around the park next to the lake and I found solid metal plates underground. There's just an old clock tower there, so you wouldn't expect it to have such a strong protected wall to its basement. I wonder if it might be a clue.'

'Interesting,' said Mickey. 'We don't have any other leads to follow and time is running out, so I say we follow Rowan and check the tower out.'

'How much longer do we have on the timer?' asked Astrid.

Mickey checked.

'AAAAARGH,' said Tilda. 'Sorry, but that's not long.'

'Then let's do the only thing we can do,' said Mickey. 'Let's get going!'

Chapter 18

'Do you really think we can get inside?' asked Astrid, as they made their way through the empty park towards the lake. It was dusk, and the park was deserted, but they were careful as ever to keep to the shadows and keep out of human sight.

'Yes!' said Mickey, trying to keep everyone's hopes up. 'It's impossible for adult humans to break in but we're a girl, a sloth, a spider monkey, a cat, a cobra, and a troop of moles—let's go!' She hoped she sounded more confident than she felt on the inside. If Hildegarde planned for the vault to be impossible to break into there was a high chance they would fail. But Mickey knew she had the best team beside her and they had to try.

It was important to make sure every move they made was the correct one. Mickey checked with the owls who were coordinating the birds to look for Harry either in or out of disguise; his height was something he'd struggle to disguise in any case. So far the moles were behaving perfectly, and being kept in line by Phyllis.

'Do you know, I think they really have been ruffled by what's happened to Rupert,' whispered Astrid. 'I think we can trust them.'

'We can use their help, but we must be careful,' said Mickey.

'Is this really the right place?' sighed Clarke, looking around for any other buildings nearby, but there were none; the park was completely empty apart from the old stone clock tower by the riverfront. It used to be open to everyone—Mickey had run up the steep spiral steps many times before—but now it was blocked off by a large metal fence.

'How do we get through that?' asked Astrid, sizing it up to see if she could spring over it.

'There didn't used to be a fence here,' said Mickey. 'Oh, and there's a guard at the door.' She pointed at a man in a smart navy blue uniform. 'That's new.' With a sigh of relief she continued, 'we must be on the right track. We just need to find a weak point to get inside. We'll have to go over it, around it—or,' she looked at the moles, 'under it.'

'Let's do it,' cried the moles in unison and quickly dug a tunnel in the corner protected by some large shrubs. The moles worked fast, and together they just about managed to make a tunnel big enough for Mickey and her team to crawl through, emerging the other side of the fence.

'Okay, stage one complete,' whispered Mickey. '2 hours 30 minutes left—we need to get moving.'

'Ooooooh no,' said Tilda, pulling a panicked face.

'We'll make it,' said Mickey, hoping she sounded more confident than she felt.

Just then the guard seemed to change patterns and began patrolling the perimeter around the clock tower.

'Right!' said Mickey. 'There's a keypad on

the door so we need to know what the code is. Astrid, can you get close and watch the guard typing in the code when they come back?'

Astrid climbed up a tree and made her way over to the roof of the tower, peering down so she had a clear view on the keypad.

The guard completed his patrol and headed back indoors. Astrid carefully crawled back towards Mickey.

'Did you see the number?' she asked.

'387124 then the hash button that looks like a grid,' she reported.

'Good job!' said Mickey, carefully committing the code to memory. 'Now we need to get the guard to come back outside and then we need to ensure that we can get inside without the guard seeing us, or the security cameras picking us up.'

'But how?' asked Phyllis anxiously.

'Clarke,' whispered Mickey, 'you're up!'

'Do it,' Clarke said bravely, and braced himself.

Mickey took her flask of water out of her pocket and shook it over Clarke. To his

credit, he didn't make a sound but did frown
furiously as the water sprayed all over him.
His fur instantly drooped and gave him
the look of a towel that had accidentally
been dropped in the bath. He then spread a
woebegone expression on his face and let out
a tremendous

YOWL.

'Oh, you poor thing,' said the guard, coming out of the building and scooping Clarke up in his arms. 'What are you doing here? Did you fall in the water? Don't worry, we'll get you warmed up then we'll see if we can find who you belong to. You are a magnificent cat, aren't you?'

Mickey held up her right hand to signal for everyone else to stay still and quiet while Clarke was taken inside the building.

She counted another five precious minutes on the timer to give Clarke enough time to fully distract the guard and take control of the cameras then she beckoned to the others to follow her and they approached the door. She typed in '**387124#**' and heard the satisfying click as the door unlocked and she pushed it open to find a door marked 'Office' and the top of a spiral staircase leading down to the underground levels.

Mickey placed her ear against the office door and could hear Clarke miaowing away. Satisfied that he would take care of the security feeds she led the team down the winding staircase until they came to a door that was painted in glossy black paint. There didn't seem to be a lock or code to open it. Mickey reached out and tentatively tried the handle. She thought the best-case scenario would be to find the vault immediately (ideally open and with Rupert safely inside) and worst-case just a storeroom and the realization her hunch had been wrong. Mickey turned the handle and to her surprise, it opened. However, the room's contents were not what she expected at all.

It was completely empty.

Chapter

19

'That's why there's no lock on the door!' said
Mickey. 'There's nothing to steal!' And there
really was nothing in the room. The wooden
floorboards were well-polished and the
wallpaper was white with blue polka dots, but
apart from that there was nothing else except
the door they'd just stepped through.

'There's nothing here!' cried the moles,

scrabbling around all over the floor.

'What a waste of time!' said Tilda.

'Wait,' said Mickey. 'There must be something we can't see.'

'It must be the floorboards,' said Astrid. 'Maybe the moles can lift them up . . .' she trailed off, as the moles dived forward and began frantically trying to slide their paws into the gaps between them.

'Don't panic,' Mickey said, trying to stay calm. There must be something they were missing. She decided to share her favourite codebreaking tip with everyone. 'Please can everyone scan the room from left to right and up and down slowly. Can anyone see anything strange?'

'Tiny dots,' said Tilda slowly.

'What did you say?' Mickey asked.

'Dots in the dots,' Tilda replied, staring at the wallpaper.

Mickey walked up to the wall and studied the polka dot wallpaper carefully. 'Oh, well-spotted Tilda. This isn't a polka dot at all, it's a microdot!' she exclaimed. 'It's a way of hiding messages in plain sight—if you zoom in really close then you can read them like a book!

This dot says "no, no, no, no, no" in really tiny writing!'

'Do any of them say anything else?' Mickey asked. The animals scrambled to scan the room from left to right and up and down, looking at the dots.

'This one!' hissed Coby, pointing with her tail. 'It's different. It says "yes, yes, yes, yes."'

Mickey reached out and pressed the 'yes' polka dot. She heard a gentle 'click' and her heart jumped—they were on to something. As she had thought, Hildegarde's puzzle would thwart most humans—a room with polka dot wallpaper would be impossible unless you knew about microdots and were with a group of animals with exceptional eyesight. Although Mickey had heard a click, nothing else had actually happened.

'Are there any more dots with the word yes?' asked Mickey.

'Yes, I've found one,' said Astrid peering carefully at a dot near the door.

'Press it!' Mickey said, excitedly.

Astrid reached up on her tiptoes, pressed the dot and was rewarded with another satisfying 'click'. Encouraged by this, Astrid continued her search and found a third 'yes' dot. She pressed it with her tail, landed on her feet, and skidded.

Mickey thought this was odd as Astrid was usually very skilful on her feet but then she realized the third dot had unlocked a mechanism and a portion of the wall had moved aside, to reveal a dark tunnel beyond. They must be getting closer.

'Come on!' Mickey whispered urgently to the others.

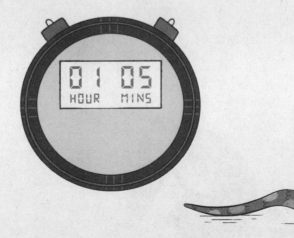

Chapter 20

Together, they crawled through the tunnel and reached another room. Mickey thought it looked like a very expensive kitchen or a very cheap spaceship. The ceiling was silver with a big metallic fan spinning around. The walls

were covered in giant mirrors, and at the far side of the room was a heavy door secured with a keypad with numbered keys lit up by a bright white light. The floor was covered in grey tiles and empty apart from a large black and white striped dining table with six grey chairs dotted around it.

Mickey scanned the room. There were no letters, no numbers, just lots of miniature Mickeys reflected in the mirrors looking back at her. This looked like her worst nightmare—a visual code, with no numbers or letters to play with. And one where her friend's life might rest on their ability to solve it.

She looked at the stopwatch. It had just ticked under one hour—59 minutes and 50 seconds to go. She forced herself to think, and told herself to think logically. There must be something they were missing.

'Why would you have a dining room underground?' pondered Astrid as she walked round the table.

'Why *wouldn't* you?' bristled the mole next to her immediately. Mickey made a note to work on the underground/above-ground relations when this case was over.

'But also,' Mickey interrupted, 'how do we open this door? There's no handle.'

'Maybe the code for the keypad is hidden in the room somewhere?' said Tilda carefully.

Mickey looked around the room again. There was almost nothing to work with except the table and chairs.

'There are 6 chairs, 1 table, and 2 ways in and out of the room,' she said slowly. 'These could be the numbers for the code, but I don't know which order they would be in or if this would be enough.'

'Keep thinking,' hissed Coby. 'How long on the timer?'

'57 minutes,' gulped Mickey.

'Oh nononononono, Rupert is doooooomed,' Tilda panicked.

'Tilda,' said Coby sternly. 'Stop that, we have a job to do.'

'Sorry,' said Tilda, but Mickey could see she was still shaking her head from side to side, but so slowly it was easy to miss. Despite the ticking clock Mickey knew you had more chance of success if you stayed calm.

'It's going to be okay,' she reassured Tilda. 'We'll figure it out.'

Tilda visibly relaxed as Mickey felt her own shoulders hunch up. In fact, she had no idea what to do next.

'Do you think it has something to do with the furniture?' asked Astrid, hanging off the end of one of the chairs by her tail.

As Mickey watched Astrid swaying from side to side she was reminded of another of her favoured codebreaking techniques—it is always worth looking at things from another angle. She sat on the floor and looked up at the table—nothing. In fact, you couldn't see the striped pattern as the table was plain underneath, so there was even less information to work with. She tried climbing on a chair and looking down at it—that didn't help either. Then she caught sight of Coby slithering round the outside of the room, tipping her head to one side then the other as she examined everything she could, and Mickey suddenly felt like a lightbulb had gone off above her head.

'Oh, I've read about these—I think this is a tilt-to-read puzzle!' she cried.

'A what?' asked Astrid.

'There was an example of one in *Cracking the Codes*! They're really clever—they don't even look like letters or numbers when you first see them but when you tilt the page the message appears. I think that's what this table is and the chairs are there to disguise it!'

'Do you want us to tilt the table?' asked the biggest mole.

'I don't know if that's neccesar . . .' Mickey trailed off, as Phyllis had quickly nodded at the other moles and they had already started building a mole pyramid against one of the table legs.

'Won't budge!' said one of the smaller moles.

Mickey walked over and gave it a shove herself, but they were right. Unlike the chairs which could be moved around the room, the table was rock solid.

'I suppose if the table can't move then we might have to tilt ourselves,' said Mickey, walking round the table to examine it more closely.

She lowered herself down, so her eyes were level with the table and scanned the table with her eyes. Nothing happened. Methodically she started working through the options—pulling herself further away from the table, from higher up then from lower down. Finally, just as she was starting to despair she caught a glimpse of something. 'Oh!' she exclaimed out loud.

'What?' asked Coby, quick on her tail.

'I think it just rearranged itself into a number, I'm sure I saw a '9'.

(PUT THE END OF YOUR NOSE HERE, LOOK DOWN AT THE PUZZLE AND TILT THE PAGE UNTIL THE WORDS APPEAR. IT MAY HELP IF YOU TRY CLOSING ONE EYE.)

She tried again then suddenly, just as she got the right angle, all of the stripes on the

table seemed to arrange themselves
into a message.

'It says THE CODE IS 2589!' she cried.

Mickey ran over and typed it into the
keypad. She held her breath, trying not
to look at the constantly ticking down
stopwatch and think about what would
happen if she was wrong, but there was
a gentle beep and a handle popped out
of the door, ready to be opened.

'Come on!' Mickey called. 'The next
room awaits!'

Chapter

A

21

The next room was bright, and even though Mickey knew they were inside, it felt like being in a garden. There were huge, powerful sun lamps on the ceiling, paintings of an outdoor courtyard on the walls, and large pot plants and trees covering nearly the entire floor. Creepers and ivy grew up the wall and long trailing plants ran along strings that were strung up along the ceiling. There was a faded sundial in the centre of the room which had winding leaves carved into it. The room felt beautiful and peaceful—which was exactly what Hildegarde liked about gardens, Mickey remembered— though she felt far from calm and relaxed right now as the timer was still ticking down and was showing only 45 minutes left. Surely, after all this time trying to track Rupert down they couldn't fall at the last hurdle?

She forced herself to breathe calmly, keeping a watchful eye on Tilda, then said in as clear a voice as she could manage, 'everyone search carefully, there must be a clue somewhere.' Her eyes darted around the room. 'Are there any words or letters or patterns?'

She scanned the room but there were just plants. Plants and the sundial. She couldn't run because there were too many plants in the way. Coby was slithering under the plants looking for clues, Astrid and Tilda swung themselves up branches to search from above, and the moles took a pot plant each and started shovelling the earth out to see if there was anything else inside the pots.

'Oh, please be careful!' Mickey cried as Astrid heaped a whole pile of soil onto the floor. And then Mickey remembered something else that Hildegard had said in the programme she had watched on TV. 'People don't stop to smell the flowers nearly often enough.'

Mickey looked around the room at the beautiful plants and remembered Hildegarde saying that some people just walked straight past plants and didn't take time to enjoy them.

She remembered Hildegarde saying in the documentary that her favourite plant was lavender because it was soothing.

Mickey made her way over to the planter that was full to bursting with lavender, ran her hands over the purple flower heads and breathed in the smell.

'Aren't you going to help us dig?' asked Tilda as she slowly removed a tiny piece of soil from a nearby plant pot.

'In a minute,' she said as calmly as she could. She moved her hands against the lavender again to free up her brain to think but then felt something hard further down next to the plant's stems. She carefully moved the flower heads aside and saw that it was a wooden plant marker but instead of saying 'lavender' (or 'Lavandula' which was its scientific name) it actually said:

BELOEMAWSYRTOREH

'What does that say?' asked Astrid, dropping lightly onto Mickey's shoulders.

'I don't know yet,' said Mickey, examining it.

'I like the spiral patterns,' said Tilda, hanging down from her branch.

'Spirals . . .' said Mickey to herself. 'Astrid, is this like the spiral code you made for me?'

Astrid's eyes lit up. 'It could be, but this is a harder version. How many letters are there?'

'Sixteen,' said Mickey, who was already doing the maths.

Mickey tried not to think about the ticking clock and instead focused on the job at hand. In the moment she forgot about the fact she was currently trapped underneath the ground on her way to the country's most expensive bank vault accompanied by more moles than she'd ever seen in her life.

She took her notebook from her pocket, took a deep breath and began her favourite trick of staring at it slowly, then moving her eyes up and down and from left to right.

She counted the letters again then carefully divided the letters into four equal groups of four and stacked them on top of each other to make a grid.

```
B  E  L  O
E  M  A  W
S  Y  R  T
O  R  E  H
```

'I've got it!' she cried, 'it IS another spiral, you just have to build the shape first. It says

BELOW THE ROSEMARY

'What's rosemary?' asked Tilda.

'Don't you know anything about gardening?' asked Mickey.

'I do,' said Phyllis. 'It's this one. I've always liked the smell.'

She patted a planter with her paw and leaned in to sniff the woody green branches. Mickey put all her weight against the pot and pushed with all her might. The big stone planter moved much more easily than she was expecting and underneath was a trapdoor. She heard a dull thud which she assumed was part of the machinery of the room getting ready to reveal its secrets.

'Come on!' she called. As she lifted it up she felt a chill blow towards her and saw the top of a metal ladder stretching down into the darkness below.

'I think we're going even further underground!' she called back to her team.

'Excellent!' cried the moles.

Chapter

22

Mickey and the animals all made it down
the ladder one by one, Coby wrapped around
Mickey again, like a giant snake scarf.

'Well, well, well,' said Coby as they all
stared at the dark room. 'Can anyone see a
lightswitch?'

'Got it,' came Phyllis's voice, as the room
lit up before them.

Finally, they were in the vault room. Gleaming wooden planks covered the floor, the walls were lined with lockers like the type you'd find at a swimming pool but much, much sturdier. There was a low bench along one wall and in the centre of the room was a gleaming black metal safe with a bright gold dial in the middle.

'The Impossible Vault!' gasped Mickey. She couldn't believe they'd got this close.

'We need to secure this room,' said Coby. 'Hopefully Clarke is still keeping the guard busy, but we can't rely on that alone. I can see three cameras. Can anyone see any more?'

'There's one down there on the floor,' said Rowan.

'Excellent. Mickey, can you power them down?' Coby asked.

Mickey was already over at one of the cameras, but it was hard-wired into the wall with no way of disconnecting it.

'I don't think we can!' she called back. 'Can

we cover them?'

She looked around the room desperately. Because the room had been in darkness, she realized that if they could cover the cameras up then whoever was watching it would hopefully think they were looking at a dark room rather than one where the cameras had been covered up. It was a good backup in case Clarke was growing tired of providing a distraction.

'If only we had something to stick over them!' she exclaimed.

'We have a lot of moles,' said Tilda thoughtfully. 'And I can cover that bigger one up there,' she said pointing at a fifth camera up on the ceiling.

'Tilda, that is a BRILLIANT idea,' said Mickey. Tilda lifted her arms and Mickey raised her up until she was level with the camera. Tilda wrapped her arms and legs around it so the lens was completely covered.

'Are you okay up there?' Astrid called up.

'Quite comfortable thank you,' came the reply.

'We'll do it too!' cried the moles.

'Thank you,' said Coby, 'though we only need four. Mickey, will you do the honours?'

Mickey set four moles on the lenses. Their limbs weren't as long as Tilda's, so they had to cling on tightly.

'That's the room secure,' said Coby, pleased. 'Now, how do we get into this safe?'

'Is there anything you can do?' Mickey asked the moles who weren't covering the cameras. They'd managed to get inside The United Bank, so she figured it was worth a try on The Impossible Vault. But sadly, Hildegarde wasn't going to be beaten that quickly.

The moles dived on the safe, some tried to burrow underneath but they couldn't prise up the floorboards. Three tried balancing on top of each other to see if there was anything interesting on top or round the side. There wasn't. One tried to eat the gold dial but took one bite and howled because it was too cold for his teeth.

Looking at the dial, Mickey felt her heart sink. She could do puzzles but there were thousands of possible options and they didn't have much time. Mickey looked at the timer and felt even worse. There were just ten minutes left.

She put her mouth against the hinge.

'Rupert?' she called softly, then louder in case he couldn't hear her. 'RUPERT? Are you there? We're here, we're going to get you out!'

'What would Hildegarde do?' asked Astrid. 'Thinking like her got us through the last room.'

She made a fair point. Even though she was worried it was a hopeless task and the dial looked so imposing she was fairly sure she wouldn't be able to crack it, Mickey decided to try.

She put her ear to the safe and turned the dial.

Silence.

She tried it again. Still nothing.

'That's strange,' she said. 'Usually they click or do something when you move the dials on the safe.' She tried wobbling it around in case that was the trick then when she pushed it from side to side it moved. She tried again, and it swung round revealing a keyhole which required a large key.

'It's not a code this time. We need a key!' she cried.

'Do we have one of those?' asked Phyllis.

'We do not,' said Coby, taking in the room.

Mickey sized up the lock. The key needed was much larger than the one she used to come and go from her flat. What she needed was something long and thin—she looked at her own arms—they would never fit inside. But then she remembered whose might.

'Astrid!' said Mickey, 'can you try your arm in the keyhole?'

'I'm a *mon*key not a key . . .'

'I know,' said Mickey, 'but it might work. Put it in here, then see if you can use your arm like a key.'

Astrid wiggled her arm around. Suddenly, there was a funny noise.

'I think something just moved,' she reported.

'Great,' said Mickey, anxiously trying not to look at the timer but painfully aware it now said there was only one minute to go.

'Try again,' Mickey encouraged, holding her breath.

Astrid frowned and wriggled her arm. There came a satisfying click and the door swung open. Mickey and Coby sprang forward

together and pulled the door open as widely
as they could. Mickey scrambled in once the
gap was big enough and looked everywhere.
But sadly, while there were shelves upon
shelves of golden storage boxes, they had no
idea which box held Rupert.

'So, you did it!' An unpleasantly familiar
voice cut through the room.

In the adrenaline rush of opening the safe,
Mickey almost missed the sound of footsteps
approaching. She spun round and saw Harry
standing at the bottom of the ladder, blocking
their exit. Troy and the other sunglasses-
wearing moles were gathered around his feet.

'Well, well,' said Harry. 'You were so clever
finding your way into this room you didn't
stop to see if anyone was following you. And
now here we are.'

He reached into his pocket and lifted out a
terrified-looking Rupert. His paws were bound
together, and his mouth was covered with a
gag, so he couldn't make a squeak.

Mickey gulped. They had come so far but
this did not look good.

Chapter
23

'YOU!' cried Mickey. 'Stay away from us!'

'Yessss,' said Coby gliding across to join her. 'What do you think you're doing?'

Harry put one hand in the air but the other held onto Rupert with a tight grip. 'Really? You were so pleased with yourselves for breaking in to the vault that you didn't think to check if anyone was behind you? Tut, tut, tut. Looks like the **COBRA** spies aren't as accomplished as you think you are. But luckily for you, I mean you no harm. In fact I think we work quite well together. And Rupert was never in any real danger, I just needed you to *think* that he was.'

'If he's not in any danger then let him go,' said Mickey.

'As you wish,' Harry replied, removing the ties then bending down to put Rupert on the floor. He immediately scuttled towards Mickey who picked him up and held him tightly against her.

'Rupert!' cried Mickey. 'Are you okay?'

'This is not my preferred state of being,' said the rat. 'Those *beasts* caught me after the bank break-in and have been moving me around disorienting underground locations ever since. I do not think I am okay, though I am much better, of course, for seeing you my dear.'

Mickey glared at Harry. Now her fears over Rupert were somewhat settled she was filled with fury that he'd been kidnapped in the first place.

'Look,' Harry said, 'I know I made a mistake leaving **COBRA** but really it was all just an unfortunate misunderstanding.'

Mickey carried on glaring at him.

'I know you don't think much of me at the moment, but I hope you remember I did good work for **COBRA** once upon a time. And to replace me with a mere *child?* Well, I have to say that is most disappointing.'

'Mickey's ten times the agent *you'll* ever

be,' said Tilda bravely, from her perch on top of the security camera.

'That's as may be, she certainly shows promise,' said Harry smiling, but Mickey noticed that it didn't spread to his eyes. 'But I really am sorry about the way things panned out.'

'What do you want Harry,' hissed Coby.

'I've come for something very precious, which is hidden in this very vault. Since leaving **COBRA** I have moved on to bigger and better things. I now work for a top-secret organisation which I hope you understand, must remain a secret to you. You should feel very lucky that I haven't told my boss about you . . . yet.'

'Oh, you're too kind,' murmured Astrid sarcastically.

'And I've been on a secret mission. This vault was built by one of the best spies of all time—*Hildegarde L. McTavish*. It had fallen into disuse until the bank bought it. They made it into a high-security vault for their most prized, and richest customers. Banking valuables here would be a signal of just how very important you were, and the bank was attracting some very good business.

'The thing is, news of the refurbishment of the vault caused quite a stir in my organisation. My boss had heard tell of some very important—priceless—documents, hidden in the vault when it was built by Hildegarde. I was tasked with getting my hands on the documents, except the bank were being frustratingly secretive about the location of the vault. And so I decided to call on my animal friends for help.'

'But you told us you wanted to help us find our own HQ!' reminded Phyllis. 'You didn't say anything about secret documents. And kidnapping Rupert was wrong!'

'I assure you the kidnap wasn't planned,' said Harry. 'I had to make some quick decisions in the field which I hoped to be able to explain to you all afterwards.'

'So you lied to us,' spluttered Troy.

'You can still use the vault as your HQ if you wish,' Harry said shrugging his shoulders.

'Rupert was an unfortunate complication,' said Harry smoothly. 'I regret he was kept quite so long but if the moles had worked faster this would all have been wrapped up much more quickly.'

There was a sharp intake of breath from the moles—both Phyllis's team and Troy's.

'I beg your pardon,' said Troy, 'that's not what you said to us. Do you know, I don't think you ever did care about above-ground/below-ground relations.'

Harry looked at the animals nonchalantly. They had been duped by Harry and it stung. Just what *was* he looking for, Mickey wondered. She turned to Coby and was pleased to see that she was also in Very Suspicious Mode.

'Well if this story stacks up you won't have any interest in any of the gold and jewels, since it is these mysterious documents you came for?'

Harry stretched up and tapped the ceiling tiles until he was rewarded with a duller 'thud'.

'Ah, hollow!' he murmured. Mickey and the animal spies and the two teams of moles watched, stunned, as Harry pressed on specific spots of the ceiling tile which then clicked and dropped down like a flap. Harry reached up and removed a dusty folder from the cavity in the ceiling. It was yellow with age and the edges of the paper were curling but not as much as Harry's lip as he lifted it down. 'So it was all true,' he murmured with delight. 'I shall be rewarded handsomely now that I have this'

Harry straightened up and turned to Coby. 'I assure you that I have no interest in anything else in this vault. I thank you for your assistance. If the security guard is any good at his job, he'll be heading down here any second. I suggest we all make a quick getaway.' Then Harry turned to Mickey. 'You have proven yourself to be an excellent spy on this mission. Why don't you work for me? I could use an apprentice . . .'

'Never!' Mickey cried.

'Very well,' Harry said. 'But don't say I didn't give you a chance to join the winning side.' He nodded to Troy who began climbing up the ladder with his gang of moles. Then with a wide grin Harry hit the light switch so the room was plunged into darkness and all Mickey, **COBRA**, and Phyllis's moles could hear was the pounding of his feet on the ladder as he left them behind—taking the precious folder with him.

Phyllis and her moles could navigate in the dark but couldn't climb the ladder to follow him, while Mickey and the animals who could climb couldn't see where the ladder was in the darkness and confusion.

Mickey fumbled around the room until she

hit on the light switch. She pulled herself up the ladder then turned and reached down. 'Come on Coby, we can catch him!' The snake met her gaze and said urgently: 'You go! You're the fastest, and we need time to reset the rooms and cover our tracks. The one thing worse than Harry's return would be for the bank to realize there had been a break-in and start investigating. **COBRA**'s existence must remain a secret at all costs!'

Mickey began to worry that Harry's headstart in the blackout had given him the advantage, but ran as fast as she could as she tore through the rooms they'd carefully cracked on the way in. Thankfully all the doors proved easier to open from the other side—the bank had clearly been concerned with break-*ins* rather than break-*outs*. But, frustratingly, as she emerged outside to be met with a clear view and no sign of Harry anywhere she realized that once again, he had got away.

She looked down at Clarke who was waiting patiently for them outside. His fur was shining in the moonlight. 'Clarke, are you wearing . . . glitter? Did the guard try to dress you up?'

'Maybe,' he said haughtily. 'Or perhaps I chose it myself.'

Chapter
24

'I can't believe that Harry duped us *again*.'
Clarke was seething back in **COBRA** HQ the
next day.

'At least we got Rupert back safely,' said
Tilda slowly. 'Who knows what Harry would
have been capable of if we hadn't found the
way into the vault.'

'I am very glad to be back; my thanks
for your excellent work under pressure my
dears,' said Rupert, who was back in his
usual seat.

'At least you weren't taken in by him as much as the moles were,' said Phyllis sadly. The majority of the moles were waiting outside but Phyllis had been permitted to join the High Committee as they debriefed the previous day's happenings. Troy and his gang of moles were currently cornered by Bertie. Coby planned to speak to them afterwards in case there was any light they might be able to shed on the recent underground escapades. The moles were also charged with thinking up a way to clear up the mess they had made.

'I wonder what was in that folder?' said Mickey.

'I too have been wondering that', said Coby. 'Whatever it was, Harry went to great lengths to get his hands on it.'

'Rupert, you are back as Head of Wild Animals but given your ordeal perhaps you might like to keep Mickey on as a Deputy Head of Wild Animals while you get back on your feet,' Coby continued. 'Would you like that?'

'I can't think of anything better,' said the

rat. 'Mickey?'

For once she didn't need to think or puzzle over the answer. There was just one word she needed, and it came to her straight away. 'YES!' she cried.

'Phyllis,' Rupert continued. 'You were a great help to me and you mustn't feel bad for being tricked by Harry; he can be very convincing.'

Phyllis nodded sadly.

'This case did throw up a problem we should have been aware of much earlier and that is the relations between under- and over-ground animals. With Coby's permission I'd like to make you my Underground Officer and we'll meet regularly to make sure we're both aware of happenings going on outside our usual habitat.'

'I agree this sounds useful,' said Coby. 'Phyllis?'

Phyllis nodded and went over to squeeze Rupert's paw. 'Of course. Thank you.'

As Mickey walked home from the meeting she didn't trip over any new molehills. True to their word Troy and his team were obviously already on the case to clean up the town. Mickey still had the uncomfortable feeling that Harry was out there somewhere. Just what would he plan next?

Their break-in at The Impossible Vault seemed to have escaped the notice of humans, although a rumour did start spreading round that a sloth had been seen on CCTV at The Impossible Vault for no reason at all. Somehow it had turned into an urban legend that one of the levels of protection for items inside The Impossible Vault was a group of highly-trained sloths.

BREAKING *NEWS*

THE BANK SAYS **THEY CANNOT CONFIRM OR DENY THE PRESENCE OF HIGHLY-TRAINED SLOTHS AT THE IMPOSSIBLE VAULT.**

Mickey was glad no one else had realized they had breached the vault, but a few days later everything changed when she bounded into the flat one day after school and saw an envelope sitting on the kitchen table. Her name and address were written out in a very neat distinctive handwriting that up to now Mickey had only seen in books. It belonged to *Hildegarde L. McTavish!*

Dear Mickey,

I received word that The Impossible Vault was recently breached and that you were the one to do it. Don't worry, you aren't in any trouble, I've heard all about how you were working to save your pet rat. He is lucky to have you. I am so pleased you have a passion for codebreaking. Perhaps you might like to meet up when I am back in the country? My travels will take me away for a few months but meeting a fellow codebreaker would bring me a great deal of joy.

Though perhaps stay away from bank break-ins in future. (Even for the best of reasons.)

Very best wishes,

Hildegarde L. McTavish

PS—and always remember that when life gives you lemons you must make lemonade!

Mickey's first thought was to wonder how on earth Hildegarde knew all this, but she quickly realized that a super spy like her could find out anything they wanted. She then had to process the idea that her hero knew all about her, had sent her encouraging words and actually wanted to meet up! She hugged the letter tightly and was immediately hit by the strong smell of lemons. That was odd. She lifted the letter and sniffed it cautiously. Hildegarde had mentioned lemonade in her last line. Mickey remembered her favourite chapter of *Cracking the Codes*, about how

Hildegarde had created her own invisible ink that could only be revealed when heat was applied. What if this was a clue?

Excited to reveal the message, Mickey ran to fetch the hairdryer and carefully held it against the paper. Her excitement quickly dropped into her stomach when new words appeared at the top of the letter. There were just two of them. And they said:

HELP ME

Mickey had finally found a real-life secret message from Hildegarde! Her brain immediately started ticking. *Hildegarde L. McTavish* needed her help. Maybe she wanted an assistant—or maybe she was in trouble. Either way, it was down to Mickey to find out. Some people might be daunted by a strange message hidden in invisible ink. But in one very important way, Michaela Rose Thompson was actually quite extraordinary. She had an extraordinary group of friends. And after cracking two

fiendishly tricky cases, Mickey
knew there was no mystery she
and the elite squad of animal spies
known as **COBRA** couldn't face
together.

About the author

Anne Miller grew up in Scotland and now lives in London where she makes TV and radio programmes including BBC Two's *QI* and Radio Four's *The Museum of Curiosity*. She reached the semi-finals of the fiendishly difficult quiz show *Only Connect* and has two *Blue Peter* badges. Her current favourite animal is a Sun Bear.

ANNE MILLER

About the illustrator

BECKA MOOR

Becka Moor is a children's book illustrator living in Manchester. She studied illustration for children's publishing at Glyndwr University, graduating in 2012. Since then, she has worked on a variety of young fiction, non-fiction & picture books. She has a slight obsession with cats and likes anything a bit on the quirky side.

PUZZLES!

Secret Spirals

Can you read the spirals and decipher the secrets?

```
            R U P E R
            M E I S T
T O P       A U R A S
E T S       N H T R M
R C E       E L D D I

      H I L D E G G
      R T O I S A
      O M A U E R
      T D A R C D
      T E L L A E
      E P A S A H
```

Advanced Spirals

Write the letters out in a grid shape, filling in the letters line by line. Then read your message in a spiral. e.g. **MICKPSOEMXNYOHTR** becomes

M I C K
P S O E
M X N Y
O H T R

Remember: The secret to writing spiral codes is you need enough letters to fit neatly into a square grid. If you don't have enough you can pad out the message by adding the number of 'X's you need at the end of your message.

PUZZLES!

Number of letters in your message	Size of grid
4	2 x 2
9	3 x 3
16	4 x 4
25	5 x 5
36	6 x 6

MORDESOCE

MICKEYANEWMWROONIIOSXXSLFNOISLKCABEB

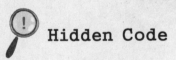 ## Hidden Code

Did you spot the hidden code within the magnifying glasses in this book?

Hint: You might want to try reading it the other way round

CATCH UP ON PAST ADVENTURES . . .

BOOK 1

Huge thanks to Lamont, Louise Lamont, Agent
Extraordinaire, for championing Mickey and the
COBRA team.

To Mickey's brilliant editor Clare Whitston and
to Emma Young, Kate Penrose, Hannah Penny, Liz
Scott, Eirian Griffiths and everyone at OUP.

To Becka Moor for capturing the mischievous
moles perfectly.

Thanks to Sarah Lloyd, John Lloyd and
everyone at QI for making life Quite Interesting,
and to the GCHQ 'Top Secret' exhibition for code
inspiration.

To my friends Robin Stevens for reading early
drafts and invaluable insights, Edward Brooke-
Hitching for Talpidae advice, and Ben, Sara, Mira,
Adam, Cynthia, James and Joe for everything.

To my parents for a childhood filled with
stories, to my brother Alasdair for the best-timed
visit to an owl centre of all time and to my husband
Sam for reading endless drafts and making
everything a joy.

And to the readers and booksellers who have
embraced the world of animal spies – I hope you
enjoy meeting the moles!

ANNE MILLER